Books by Ross MacKenzie

The *Nowhere Emporium* Trilogy:
The Nowhere Emporium
The Elsewhere Emporium
The Otherwhere Emporium

Shadowsmith

Evernight

THE OTHERWHERE EMPORIUM

ROSS MACKENZIE

Kelpies

Kelpies is an imprint of Floris Books
First published in 2020 by Floris Books
© 2020 Ross MacKenzie

Ross MacKenzie has asserted his right
under the Copyright, Designs and Patent Act 1988
to be identified as the Author of this Work
All rights reserved. No part of this book may be
reproduced without the prior permission of
Floris Books, Edinburgh www.florisbooks.co.uk
British Library CIP data available
ISBN 978-178250-663-8
Printed and bound by MBM Print SCS Ltd, Glasgow

MIX
Paper from
responsible sources
FSC® C117931

Also available as an eBook

Floris Books supports sustainable forest management by
printing this book on materials made from wood that comes
from responsible sources and reclaimed material

For Colin and Amanda

CHAPTER 1
THE IMPOSSIBLE SHOP

Elmbank, near Glasgow, Present Day

Mrs Susan Feather dashed along Elmbank High Street, laden with shopping bags, her collar turned up against the late November wind. As she waited at the traffic lights, she glanced up at the clock face on the gothic tower of the town hall. Three o'clock. Mirren would be home from school in an hour, and Susan wanted to have the bolognese bubbling on the stove when her daughter got back. Thursday was spag bol night, and Susan knew Mirren loved the smell of garlic and tomato and onion and basil to greet her when she came through the door.

As the lights began to change from green to amber,

a silver van sped up to make it through the junction, tearing through a puddle, throwing up a curtain of dirty water that soaked Susan from the waist down.

"Aye, thanks, pal!" she yelled after the van as it sped away. The green man flashed on, and Susan hurried in a diagonal across the street, swearing under her breath at the van driver. Her shoes were soaked, *squelch-squelching* with every step, past the bank and the estate agents until, at last, she reached the doorway to the flat, put down her bags and fumbled in her coat pockets for the key. Then it was into the close, dim in the darkening afternoon, smelling of the bleach she'd used to clean the landing that morning, and up two flights of stairs to the front door.

Key in the lock, *rattle rattle*, door open, *creak creak*, and she was back in the warmth of the flat, the familiar smell of Mirren's favourite candle, Winter Berries, all sweet and spicy, still in the air. Five minutes later, Susan was in a dry pair of trousers and humming along to classic rock tunes on the radio while she unpacked the shopping.

"I don't believe it," she said, rubbing her face wearily. "I've only gone and forgotten the bloomin' spaghetti!" She checked the bags again, hoping that a packet of spaghetti might suddenly materialise. No such luck. With a sigh she went to the hall, slipped on her coat, headed out the front door, down the stairs, and out into the autumn cold.

Susan hurried along the street towards the corner shop, hands stuffed in her pockets, breath fogging, muttering at her own forgetfulness.

And then she stopped.

She looked at the row of shops to her right.

There was Bannantyne's, the butchers, as usual.

And the newsagents too. Nothing strange there.

What *was* strange – very strange indeed – was the shop that sat *between* Bannantyne's and the newsagents.

The store in question was made of shining black bricks, bricks the colour of midnight that sparkled in the blood-orange light of the setting sun. The doorway was a tall narrow archway, the top of which was a seven-pointed star. And above it was a golden sign that might, at some point in the distant past, have been grand, but was now faded.

Susan moved closer. She walked right up to the shop, reached out and touched the cold shining bricks.

They felt real. They felt… familiar…

But they couldn't be, could they?

Because this shop, the Nowhere Emporium, had simply not been here this morning. Susan was sure of it. And the reason she was so sure – as certain as a person can possibly be – was because there was *no shop* between Bannantyne's and the newsagents.

It was a strange feeling, knowing that something was impossible and yet seeing it right in front of your eyes.

I need to get to the corner shop, she thought. *Need to get the spaghetti for Mirren's dinner.*

But the Nowhere Emporium… it was calling her. Pulling her in.

She took a step towards the door, and another, and the closer she got, the more she felt like a helpless fish on an angler's hook. She reached for the door handle, and when her fingers closed around it, it was like touching ice. She pulled back her hand, examined her palm, and then reached out again, grasping the handle, opening the door.

A breath of warm air brushed over her. She inhaled deeply. Rich, familiar scents of melting chocolate and Christmas spices and new books ensnared her, seemed to reach out and wrap a gentle arm around her, and before she knew what was happening, she was walking through the door.

From the very first glance inside, Susan Feather knew that this was like no shop she had ever seen.

It was dim and dusty, lit only by the weak light from the dirty window and the warm flickering glow of a spitting fire. What little light there was gleamed and danced on the countless treasures upon the shelves and display cabinets. It shone on gold-leaf letters on the spines of ancient books. It played on the faultlessly cut surfaces of diamonds and rubies and sapphires. It reflected on the countless clocks and mirrors on the walls and made the eyes of stuffed animals glow bright in the gloom.

Susan wandered around like she was in a dream, picking up toy soldiers and pocket watches and daggers with handles of polished bone. She stroked the fur of a polar bear and stared into a tank of iridescent fish, and when she dipped her fingers in the water the inhabitants swam up and nibbled at her fingertips.

"Susan."

She drew her hand out of the fish tank with a jerk, looked around, saw nobody. "Hello?"

"Hello, Susan." The voice was deep and silky, and somehow seemed to be all around her.

"Who's there?" Susan suddenly felt not at all like an adult, but like a small, frightened girl.

"A friend, Susan. Someone who wants to help."

Susan frowned. "Help? Help how?"

"It's difficult being a parent, isn't it?" the voice went on. "Especially a single parent. I was one myself once.

We love our children, of course, but oh what we wouldn't give, Susan, for a taste of the freedom we used to enjoy. Don't you agree?"

Susan took a step back. "Erm… look, I don't know who you are, or what this place is, but I don't think I should be here. I have to get back to my daughter…"

"Of course," said the voice. "Of course you do." The door to the shop swung open of its own volition, and in swept a rush of cold, damp air. Rain was now falling in great fat drops, battering the street outside.

Susan took a few steps towards the door, but another blast of that deliciously warm shop air, infused with its beguiling scents, closed around her like a gentle hand and turned her around, and she noticed for the first time a red velvet curtain at the back of the shop. She watched the folds open slightly, caught a glimpse of something bright and shining beyond.

"Before you go," said the deep voice again, "why don't you take a quick look behind the curtain? It won't take more than five minutes, and I promise you it'll be worth it."

Susan stood very still, her gaze falling upon the curtain. "Is this magic?" she asked, realising, as the words left her mouth, how childlike they sounded. But that's exactly how she felt: like she was eight years old again, ready to believe in the impossible.

"Yes," said the voice. "It's magic. Behind that curtain, Susan, you will find Wonders beyond anything you've ever imagined. What harm could there be in taking a look? Five minutes, that's all. And if you like it, why not bring your daughter back later? Mirren is her name, yes?"

Another frown. "Yes, that's her name. But I don't remember telling you that." Susan edged closer to the curtain. The grown-up in her, the mother, wanted to leave. But this shop had brought out a side of her that she had buried long ago, when life and responsibility had forced her to put away childish things. Now the child in her was back and winning the argument. "I suppose it wouldn't hurt. Just a quick look. But then I have to get the spaghetti."

She moved so close to the curtain that she could reach out and touch it; the velvet was heavy and smooth, and when her fingers brushed against it, a strange charge flowed through her veins, made her stomach leap with excitement. Again, she felt that sense of familiarity; that somehow, she had been here before.

"Psst."

Susan drew back her hand, looked around.

"Psst. Over here. No, not that way. Up here! Quick!"

This was a new voice, somewhere between that of a man and a boy. Susan glanced up, saw a leathery-looking little head hanging on a string over the red curtain. It looked as if at one time it might have been human, but it was now shrivelled and shrunken, its skin cracked. A large piercing through the centre of its nose reflected the firelight. Susan stared up at it, her hand pressed to her chest. She hoped that this tiny head had never belonged to an actual person. "Did you… did you just speak?"

The shrunken head's lips had been sewn shut, but the threads were loose, and it moved its jaw from side to side to loosen them further. "Mm. That's better. I don't have much time. I'm holding him back, but he's strong."

"Who is?" asked Susan. She was quite revolted by this object but could not look away.

"No time to explain," replied the head. "Just, please, Susan, get out of the shop. Don't go through the curtain. Don't go through any of the doors. If you do, you'll be—"

The shrunken head suddenly stopped talking. The threads through its lips had begun to tighten back up, clamping its mouth shut, until it could do nothing but make weak muffled moans.

"Don't listen to him," said the original, deep voice. "He's a troublemaker. Where were we? Ah, yes…"

From behind the curtain, she heard the sound of something small hitting the floor, and out into the shop rolled a golden coin. It stopped right in front of

Susan and spun, then came to rest. She bent over and picked it up. It was heavy. Real gold. She stared at it, turned it in her fingers. How much must it be worth?

"You can keep it if you like," said the voice. "I know how tight things are for you at home. Providing for a growing girl is an expensive business – all those new clothes. And now she wants the same trendy trainers as everyone else!"

Susan stared at the coin. "I can't take this."

"Oh, but I insist, and there's more. Come through the curtain and see…"

The shrunken head was still mumbling, but Susan was no longer paying it any attention; she had been dazzled, bewitched by this place. She swallowed, put the coin in her coat pocket, and went to the curtain. Then, her heart pounding, she pushed through.

CHAPTER 2
THE PALACE

Elmbank, near Glasgow, Present Day

It was impossible.

Susan stood, arms loose by her sides, looking all around her. *How can this be?*

When Mirren was little, Susan had read her fairy tales and bedtime stories, and in those stories, there had been kings and queens and palaces and treasure. But never, even in the wildest parts of her imagination, had Susan ever pictured a room as vast and grand as this.

She stood in the central chamber of a throne room. Either side of her, rows of unimaginably large columns reached up, seemingly forever, supporting an uncountable number of floors all honeycombed with passageways. The floor and stairways were fashioned from the finest marble; the banisters and railings gleamed gold. Everywhere she looked, Susan saw treasure: mountains of twinkling coins and emeralds and rubies; diamond diadems and brooches encrusted with precious jewels the size of robins' eggs. Suits of shining armour, paintings in gilded frames, ancient chests overflowing with pearls.

Straight ahead was an arched stained-glass window, hundreds of feet tall, depicting a giant dressed in a midnight-blue suit. He was holding a book aloft, and there were crowds of people bowing before him. At the foot of the window was an enormous throne. The warm air was heavily perfumed with orange zest and cinnamon, but beneath lingered a layer of something else, something sweet and rotten.

"Welcome, Susan." Until that moment, the throne had been empty. Susan knew this to be true. Now a man sat upon it, and he was three times the size of any human. He was dressed in what seemed to Susan to be Victorian-style clothing: a long coat and a midnight-blue suit, and atop his head perched a top hat. A leather-bound book sat open on his lap. Susan recognised him at once as the man depicted in the stained-glass window. Out in the shop his voice had been deep and rich, but here, beyond the curtain, it was so booming that Susan felt it in her bones.

It was, she thought, how a mountain might sound if mountains could speak.

"What do you think?"

Susan found her voice, but it was shaky. "W-who are you?"

The giant man closed his book, stood up. Susan noticed that when he moved, his form became undefined at the edges, swirling in smoky patterns the way ink did in water. He raised a hand, swept it around the room. When he smiled, the features of his face blurred before reforming into focus. His teeth were dazzling, and his ice-blue eyes shone with burning fire and strength. The very air around him seemed to crackle with a strange current.

"I am the master of the Nowhere Emporium. Please, Susan, have a look around."

CHAPTER 3

A CALL IN THE NIGHT

Elmbank, near Glasgow, Present Day

When the school bell rang for home time at half past three that afternoon, a great tide of jubilant children came rushing out of the doors of Elmbank Primary School, yelling and laughing and cheering the fact that this was a holiday weekend, so there would be no school for four whole days.

Mirren Feather walked among the happiness, quiet and sullen. She waited at the school gate, her eyes flicking around the many faces in the crowd, watching them thin out and eventually disappear, until she was one of only a few stragglers left. No sign of Luke. She sighed. He must have gone home another way, or managed to sneak past her – and who could blame him for avoiding her?

Mirren took her phone from her pocket, quickly typed one word and sent a text to her best friend:

Sorry

She turned and began the walk towards the centre of town and home. As she went, a quick stab of pain radiated below her left shoulder. Dr Patel at the hospital called her little arm a 'residual limb', which she did not like – she thought it made her sound like some sort of robot. Mum knew this, and so any time Dr Patel said the two dreaded words, she'd roll her eyes and make a face behind his back. It had got to the point that Mirren's twice-annual visits to hospital had become an exercise in doing her best to hold in an almighty series of giggles.

Her left arm hurt today though; even years after the accident, nerve pain would sometimes strike. It had happened a lot when she was little; some of her earliest memories were of tears and painful, sleepless nights. And of crying for her dad. She'd been too young back then to understand that Dad would not come, no matter how much she asked. Because, as well as taking most of her left arm, the crash had stolen him away too, and that caused a different kind of pain.

Her thoughts returned to Luke, and what had happened at lunch.

They'd been out in the playground, sitting together in their favourite spot at one of the picnic benches beneath the horse chestnut trees, surrounded by crisp fallen leaves and empty conker shells.

"Hey," she'd said, "did you see Danny T uploaded a new video last night? He made it all the way to the end of *Zombie Knightmare* without losing a life!"

At this, Lukasz Zajac, Mirren's best friend since Primary One, had sat forward, a half-eaten red apple forgotten in his hand, and blown the mousy brown hair from his eyes. "No. Way. That's impossible!"

"I'm telling you," Mirren had said, scraping the last of her orange yogurt from the pot. "He did! I saw it—"

"Alright, weirdos?"

At the sound of this voice, Mirren and Luke had given each other a 'here we go again' glance and turned to see Robyn Prince approaching the picnic bench, flanked by her usual gaggle of followers.

"Hi Robyn," Mirren had said. "What's up?"

"Oh, nothing much. Just wanted to show you my trainers – brand-new High Jumps!"

Mirren had looked at Robyn's feet, which were nestled in huge white and silver monstrosities that wouldn't have looked out of place on the International Space Station. "Nice."

"Nice?" Robyn had sneered. "*Nice?* These babies have got fifteen air cushions and self-tightening, glow-in-the-dark laces! My dad brought them back from America. You can't even get them in the shops here yet."

"They're really cool," Luke had told her. "But we were sort of having a private conversation before you came over."

Robyn's eyebrows had shot up. "Oh, really? Private, eh? You two planning your wedding? Ha!" She'd looked around, and her little gang had laughed on cue.

"You're not funny, Robyn," Luke had said.

Mirren had sensed him getting riled. "Leave it, Luke."

"No, I won't. She thinks she can just say what she wants. She can't!"

"Oh," Robyn had said. "Who's going to stop me? You? Like I'd listen to anything you have to say, Puke."

"Don't call me Puke. My name is Luke."

"I'll call you what I like! And Puke's a pretty good name for you, considering how disgusting you are. Look at those clothes! Do you actually own anything new, or has it all come from your loser big brother? Look at your trainers. There's a hole in the toe of one of them! How can you leave the house looking like that? Answer me, Puke!"

"Shut up!" Luke had yelled.

"Oh, poor Puke's all upset!" one of Robyn's gang had jeered.

"He looks like he's going to cry!"

"Don't cry, Puke!"

"Little baby Puke!"

Mirren almost snapped. She had glared at Robyn, had been about to say something when Robyn cut her off.

"What's *your* problem? Is it because I've upset your boyfriend? I'm sorry. Let's shake and make up, hm?" She'd held out her left hand, knowing full well that Mirren did not have one. Then she'd looked down and pretended to be surprised. "Oh, sorry! How daft of me." And she'd swapped hands, holding her right out instead with a smirk. "No? Don't want to shake? Rude."

As Robyn's pals had giggled, Mirren had felt herself shrink back. She was trembling, with anger and embarrassment.

Robyn had held up her hands, quieting her followers. "You smell that?" She'd screwed up her face, sniffed at the air, taken a few steps towards Luke. "It smells like… puke!"

"Puke! Puke! Puke!"

Mirren had looked into her best friend's eyes and seen that he was about to cry. He had stared at her, his face so sad, begging her to help him.

And Mirren had looked away. She had been too tired to fight today.

She hadn't stood up for him. She'd just hung her head and let Robyn and her gang continue to chant until poor Luke had run away across the playground.

Now, as she trudged through the posh housing estate where Robyn Prince lived, towards the towering town hall, Mirren was angry with herself. Why hadn't she done anything? If it had been the other way around and Robyn had been bullying Mirren, she had no doubt Luke would have made her stop, or at least tried. She felt ashamed. She felt like a coward.

It was almost dark by the time she got home. The smell of autumn was thick in the air, crisp and fiery. The sky was purple-blue, and the first stars were softly twinkling. Mirren reached the door of the close and rang the buzzer to the flat.

No answer.

She tried again.

Still nothing.

She took a few steps back, looked up to the flat's kitchen window and saw that the light was on. Mum must be cooking dinner with the radio turned up, she supposed. She reached into her pocket and brought out her house key. Eleven was too young to be home alone for very long, but Mum had to work crazy shifts to pay the bills, and so the key – and the fact that Mirren would sometimes spend the night in the flat alone when Mum worked nights – was their little secret. Besides, Mrs Patterson was always across the hall should Mirren need anything.

She opened the door, the pain in her arm easing. Then she let herself into the flat.

"I'm home, Mum."

She'd expected to hear her mum's rock music blaring, to smell bolognese cooking, to be greeted with a hug.

But none of those things happened.

"Mum?" Mirren checked the kitchen first, saw the unpacked ingredients sitting on the countertop. "Mum, are you here?" She went to the living room, and her mum's bedroom, and the bathroom. She even checked her own bedroom, wondering if her mum had finally cracked and gone in to tidy it.

No Mum.

Mirren did not panic.

This had happened once or twice before; work had probably called and asked Mum to start her shift early, and of course she would have said yes. They couldn't afford to turn down extra money. But it was unlike her not to leave a note on the magnetic chalkboard on the fridge or send a text. She must have been in a hurry.

Mirren locked the front door, turned on the television, and set about making herself some dinner. She couldn't cook bolognese, but she did a mean microwaved frozen mac and cheese. She ate dinner, did her homework, and then sat at her desk for a while and played video games. Mum had bought her a new gaming mouse for her last birthday, and it was a real peach! With one hand, Mirren could play video games better than anyone else she knew, and this new mouse had only helped improve what Luke called her 'mad skills'. After a while, she curled up on the couch to watch some TV. There was no school tomorrow, so she decided to stay up a bit later than usual.

She woke up on the couch some hours later, her chin covered in drool and her left leg tingling with pins and needles from the way she'd been lying. The wall clock said one in the morning. The first thing she did was check her phone to see if Mum had called or left a message, or if Luke had sent a text back. Nothing.

She'll text when she's on her break, she thought sleepily to herself. *Nothing to worry about, Mirren. Go to bed.*

Five minutes later she was curled up beneath her duvet with freshly brushed teeth and the night light on. She always used the night light when Mum worked nights. Though she drifted easily off to sleep, somewhere in the back rooms of Mirren's mind, something was beginning to bother her.

Mirren awakened in the middle of the night to the sound of a familiar ringtone – the theme tune from *Harry Potter*. Still half-asleep and confused, she reached for her bedside table, fumbled for the phone, and stared through half-shut eyes at the blindingly bright screen. She had fully expected to see Mum's number on the display, alongside the goofy picture they'd taken together on the beach in St Andrews last summer.

Instead, the screen was blank, save for a strange number.

Not Mum. Not even Luke.

Someone else. A weird caller ID that made her think she was still asleep, that this was a dream:

Nowhere

Decline   Answer

CHAPTER 4
A STRANGE OCCURRENCE

Dubrovnik, Croatia, July 1989

In the back streets of Dubrovnik Old Town, on a stifling summer night, something incredible was happening. The neighbourhood had been abuzz all that hot, sticky day with chatter of a strange shop. The shop, they said, had appeared on one of the narrow winding alleys near the Old Town walls. The shop itself was made of sparkling black brick. The doorway was an arch, closed off by a gate of finely spun gold. And above the door, a sign. Eighteen golden letters gleamed in the rays of the Croatian sun:

THE NOWHERE EMPORIUM

"Did you hear?" the people chattered among the market stalls. "It came as if from nowhere."

"It was not there yesterday…"

"I heard you can see strange-coloured light through the dirty window."

"My son says he walked past it this morning and his hair stood on end."

"Really?"

"I wonder what's inside?"

"I wonder *who's* inside!"

And so on…

Inside the mysterious shop, Daniel Holmes, proprietor of the Nowhere Emporium, sat at his grand desk, his attention fully focussed on the page upon which he was writing.

As the nib of his golden pen scratched across the thick paper, Daniel gave a contented smile. Of all the incredible ways the Emporium had changed his life, all the places he'd been and the things he'd seen, this was still his favourite part. This was the heart of everything. The letters he was forming, you see, were not simply splotches of black ink. They were so much more than that. They were *magic*. Everything Daniel wrote in the infinite pages of his *Book of Wonders* became reality somewhere in the Emporium – a new Wonder to discover. Every mark, every inky swirl, crackled with a magic that made his heart dance.

Today he was writing a Wonder that would contain a vast grassy plane, and on that plane would be, to the amazement of his customers, a great number of peacefully grazing dinosaurs.

Daniel had done his research in preparation of this Wonder. He had visited museums and archaeological digs across the world, taking pictures, speaking to experts whenever they'd entertain him. And then he had realised, in a moment of clarity one sunny afternoon, that, *theoretically*, there was nothing to stop him taking the Emporium all the way back in time to when the dinosaurs were actually roaming around.

Only…

Only, when he'd tried it, the Emporium had shaken and rumbled, and a great feeling of weakness had come over Daniel. It had been the first time such a thing had happened since he'd taken over the shop from Mr Lucien Silver a few years ago.

The first time the Emporium had not done as he had instructed.

The first time he had failed.

No matter. It was done now. Daniel put down his pen and sat back in his chair, the fire spitting in the darkened shop, its flames reflecting in the many treasures so tightly packed into the place. He picked up the *Book of Wonders* and admired his work, the detail and description. This… this would be one of his finest Wonders yet. All that was left to do – the final part of the process – was to close the book. When that happened, when those pages touched, the magic would be complete. The Wonder would appear somewhere in the great Carnival of Wonders behind the red curtain by Daniel's desk.

Scanning the work one more time, he gave a nod of satisfaction and closed the book with a snap.

He waited.

He sat forward.

He stared at the book through narrowed eyes. His heart had begun to pick up pace, and the feeling that something was wrong sat heavy and cold in his belly. Still clutching the *Book of Wonders*, he shot to his feet and wheeled away through the curtain.

"Daniel!"

"Hello, Mr Holmes!"

"Good day, Daniel! All set for opening time?"

"Master Holmes! When you have a moment,

I'd like to talk to you about my Wonder. I think we could do with a few more elephants..."

These were the voices of the Emporium staff, all of them characters written in the *Book of Wonders*, brought to life inside the Emporium by the powerful magic of Daniel's imagination. Normally, Daniel would have greeted each of them in turn, taken time to answer their questions and hear what they had to say, but today he rushed past, ignoring their calls, not seeing the puzzled looks on their faces as he went by.

At last, after goodness knows how long hurrying through the great tent city that comprised the Carnival of Wonders, between tents as tall as ten-storey buildings and tents as small as phone boxes, all under an impossible twilight sky, Daniel came around a corner and skidded to a halt on the dry summer grass.

His arms dropped to his sides, his right hand still gripping the book. His head tilted slightly to the left as his eyes surveyed the scene.

There, between two enormous tents – one of rich purple silk, the other of gold and black velvet – was the new Wonder. The new tent, however, was not shining and splendid as newly born Wonders usually were. It was small and plain and lopsided. It looked sad.

Daniel moved slowly towards the tent. When he reached the curtained entrance, he stopped and touched the worn canvas. Holding his breath, Daniel brushed the curtain aside and entered.

He should have been standing in a vast plain during the Cretaceous period, surrounded by huge, plant-eating dinosaurs.

Instead, he found himself in a bare, cold attic room. Cobweb strands hung from the ceiling and coated the small window. The floorboards were warped and dusty and creaking. The flowery, faded wallpaper was peeling from the walls. There was no furniture, no boxes or shelves. Nothing.

The only feature was a door in the far wall of the room.

Daniel's eyes scanned the door. There was nothing special about it. It was, by the look of it, a normal door – the sort you might find in any house. And yet it made him uneasy. This whole room made him uneasy.

He turned to leave.

Then he stopped and spun around.

Had he just heard...?

Was someone *behind* that door?

Daniel stood still as death, listening, waiting. No sound came. No movement. He edged across the room. When he reached the door, he realised that he was clutching the *Book of Wonders* tight to his chest, the way a child hugs a security blanket or a soft toy.

He stood inches from the door, so close that his nose was almost touching it, and he listened.

Still nothing.

He could not shake the feeling, though, that there was someone on the other side.

"Hello?" Daniel's voice sounded strange to him, shaky and hesitant. "Is someone there?"

No reply.

Daniel reached out a trembling hand, wrapped his fingers around the door handle.

A stab of icy dread pierced his heart. He gasped, staggered back to the entrance, panting as the feeling subsided. In a few moments, his senses had properly returned, and he spun away and out of the tent, back to the warm evening air of the Carnival of Wonders. There he stood, his face turned to the sky, his eyes closed, breathing deeply.

CHAPTER 5
ALL TOO MUCH

Dubrovnik, Croatia, July 1989

"Daniel?"

"Mr Daniel, are you OK?"

The voices brought him back to the here and now, and he turned and saw Caleb the fire-breather and the Ringmaster from the Iron Circus hurrying towards him. Caleb was bare-chested and bearlike, with a huge bald head. The Ringmaster, whom Daniel had struggled to name for so long before finally christening him Ted, was made entirely of metal. These were two of Daniel's most trusted members of staff.

"Oh," said Daniel. "Yeah, I'm… I'm fine." He cast a glance back to the little white tent and shivered.

"It's nearly opening time. I have to get going." He brushed past them, not noticing their looks of concern, and shouted back over his shoulder, "Places everyone! It's almost time!"

A large crowd had gathered in the street outside the shop, drawn in by the strange feeling that something magical was about to happen.

"Look," said a voice near the front of the jostling throng. "Something's happening at the doorway!"

And so it was: the finely spun golden gate that guarded the arched doorway turned to sparkling dust, scattering away into the night air.

"Look there! The door is opening!"

It opened silently, and from the darkness within came scents that ensnared the crowd even further: tantalising aromas of bonfires and autumn leaves, pine trees and roasting chestnuts.

"Someone's coming out!"

"It's a boy…"

The boy was, perhaps, in his early teens, with milk-bottle-pale skin and messy red hair. He wore a smart black suit with a golden tie.

Silence from the crowd. Absolute silence.

The boy frowned. "Well, this is no good. I can't see you all. Hold on." He snapped his fingers. The audience gasped and stepped back as a huge oak tree made entirely of light burst from the street and carried the red-haired boy gently upward between its branches. He gazed down at them, standing on a thick branch, leaning casually on the trunk. "That's better." He cleared his throat. "Dear guests, I welcome you all to my Nowhere Emporium! Through these doors you will find countless Wonders – some containing entire worlds and others single objects, but all entirely magical. Please come in, look around, enjoy. Lighten your hearts. I ask only that you bring your imagination!"

The tree exploded in a shower of golden light, and when the smoke had cleared the boy was gone. After a long moment, the crowd began to cheer and whistle. One by one, and then in eager groups, they entered the shop from nowhere.

Daniel watched his customers walk the great Carnival of Wonders, smiling as they discovered the many magical creations that lay in wait inside each tent. Too many to visit in a single lifetime, of course, but people tended to find the Wonder they needed to see most, the one that might make them happier, help conquer a fear, or boost their confidence. There was the Room of Secrets, for instance, where someone could leave a secret inside a snow globe and there it would stay, safe and sound, forever. Or the Pirate Ship, where a customer could join Captain Jean Reynard's pirate crew and sample swashbuckling life on the high seas. And of course, the Leap of Faith was always a favourite. There, a customer would step blindly into a dark room only to suddenly find that they were flying through the night sky like Peter Pan.

Between the tents, Daniel's staff entertained passers-by.

"Look at that, Daddy!" shouted a little girl, pointing towards Caleb as he made the flames from his torch take the shape of an elephant. "Look at the man breathing fire!"

Anja, the snake charmer, would enchant with her many performing snakes, and Ted's Iron Circus, where everything was made of metal, was always a hit.

Seeing people interact with his creations usually recharged Daniel, made him feel alive, content, happy. But tonight, when the last customer had left, he did not feel that way at all.

"You look exhausted, Daniel," said Ted.

"I'm fine."

"You don't look fine." Ted's face was made up of many gears and cogs and shifting metal pins. His eyes were two circles of glass, and behind them shone a warm yellow light.

"Indeed," agreed Caleb, the gentle giant. "You look like you've seen a ghost."

Daniel rubbed his eyes. He was suddenly feeling very tired. "Something went a bit wrong when I wrote in the book earlier, that's all." But that wasn't all. Something bigger was happening, he could feel it in the air. "I tried to write a Wonder, but the tent that appeared wasn't what I imagined. Come on, I'll show you…" He led them through the now empty Carnival of Wonders to the plain little tent.

No. Not to the tent. To the spot where the tent *should* have been.

"It's gone!"

Ted and Caleb shared a worried look.

"What is, Daniel? What's gone?"

Daniel rushed over to the space where the tent had been. "But that's not possible… it was right here!"

"What was there, Mr Daniel?"

"The tent! Didn't you see it? I wrote a new Wonder and it appeared, but it was all wrong. Now it's gone! But that can't happen." He opened the *Book of Wonders* and began a frantic search through the pages. "This isn't right. This can't be right. It's not in here!" Heavy panic swirled in his guts; it was a strange and foreign feeling. Here, in the Emporium, Daniel was used to being in control. Now, it seemed that he was not.

Ted's metal hands grabbed him gently by the shoulders, turned him so that he was looking up into the clockwork man's face, into those warm, glowing circles of glass. "Mr Daniel, you have to calm down. Breathe. In and out. Slowly."

"Breathe," repeated Daniel. "Yeah. Yeah, good idea. I have to breathe." He did, and began to feel a little better.

"Alright," said Caleb. "Now, without panicking, try and tell us what happened."

Daniel told them about the tent, and the room, and the door. When he was done, he waited for someone to speak. "Well? What do you think?"

A pause. Then Caleb said, "Truly?"

"Yes, of course truly."

"Truly… we think that you are very tired, Daniel. We – the staff – feel that you have been running this place alone for far too long."

"I can handle it." Daniel tried to sound defiant, but he heard the weariness in his own voice.

"How long has it been since Ellie left?" asked Caleb.

"Three years," said Ted.

Daniel shook his head. "Can it really be that long?"

Ted nodded. "When was the last time you spoke to her?"

Daniel rubbed his chin, felt the first shoots of fluffy stubble on his face. He was fifteen years old, tall and gangly, with arms and legs that seemed too long for his body. Ellie Silver was the daughter of Lucien Silver – the original owner of the Emporium. She had been like a sister to Daniel, and a great help running the shop, but she had left to pursue a career with the Bureau of Magical Investigation, hunting monsters and magical threats in London. He missed her, but he was very proud that she was out in the world making a life for herself. "She's so busy. She always makes me feel welcome whenever I visit, of course, but I feel like I'm getting in the way."

"You need company, Daniel," said Caleb. "You're lonely."

"I have you two," Daniel insisted. "And the rest of the staff."

"It's not the same as having someone from the outside world though, is it, Mr Daniel?" The cogs and pins of Ted's face had arranged themselves into an expression of compassion. "We're worried you might be starting to lose touch with the real world."

Daniel let out a snort. "That's just daft. Course I'm not losing touch. There are people from the outside world in the shop every day."

"But you don't get to know any of them, do you?" said Caleb. "They are not friends."

"You're tired, Mr Daniel," said Ted. "Running the Nowhere Emporium takes up every moment of your time, every ounce of your energy. It would eventually be too much for anyone. It even grew too big a job for Mr Silver in time, didn't it?"

"Look at what happened tonight," said Caleb. "The incident with the malfunctioning Wonder probably occurred because you are so exhausted."

Daniel nodded. "Maybe you're right."

"At last he's beginning to see sense!" Ted clapped Daniel on the back.

"You should find someone to help you," said Caleb.

Daniel frowned. "Like an apprentice?"

"Why not? Even the great Mr Silver took on an apprentice." Caleb smiled at Daniel. "And as I recall, that worked out alright."

Daniel told them he'd think on it. Perhaps he *was* just tired, but he could not shake the feeling that someone was watching him, that everywhere he went, an unseen pursuer was only a step or two away, waiting in the shadows.

His instincts told him that something was badly wrong in the Emporium.

His instincts were right.

CHAPTER 6

THE WHITE FEATHER

Elmbank, near Glasgow, Present Day

Mirren continued to stare at the strange caller ID flashing on the screen of her phone:

Nowhere

Was this a prank call? She tried letting it ring until the caller either hung up or the answerphone kicked in. Neither of those things happened. After a few minutes, the phone was still ringing and vibrating, even after she'd tried to switch it off.

Seemingly with no other choice, Mirren Feather put the phone to her ear and answered the call.

"Hello?"

A pause. The line was bad.

"Hello?" Mirren repeated.

Another pause, and the hiss of faraway static. Then someone answered.

"Mirren?" said a male voice.

Mirren sat up straight. "Who's this?"

"I don't have time to explain everything," said the voice. "You must listen carefully. Your mum is in trouble."

A jolt of panic. Mirren swung her legs around, sat on the edge of her bed in the soft turquoise glow of the night light.

"What's happened to Mum? Has there been an accident at work?"

The line crackled and hissed.

"She's not at work, Mirren. She's somewhere else. She's trapped in my shop and she needs your help. *I* need your help."

Mirren stood up, began to pace around the room. "What do you mean 'stuck in your shop'? Where is she? What's happened to her?"

"He's going to cut me off soon," said the voice hurriedly. "I might go at any moment. Mirren, this is going to sound mad, but please believe me when I tell you that every word I'm about to say is the absolute truth. I am a magician, a good magician. My shop, the Nowhere Emporium, has been taken over by an evil magician. He's keeping your mum prisoner."

Mirren held the phone away from her face, stared at the screen in disbelief. Then a thought occurred to her. "Oh. Very funny, Lukasz. You got me."

Another pause. The line crackled again. "Lukasz?" said the voice. "No, this isn't Lukasz."

"This isn't funny, Luke." Mirren's fear was beginning to turn to anger. "I know I should have stuck up for you yesterday at lunch. I'm sorry. But that doesn't mean you can phone me in the middle of the night and frighten the life out of me. Honestly, telling me my mum is in danger…"

"I'M NOT LUKASZ!" the voice pleaded. "Please. Just… look out of your window… Please, Mirren!"

She heard the fear, the desperation in the voice, and she knew she wasn't speaking to Lukasz. Her heart was battering against her chest. She stared at her phone until a sound from the window made her look up – a whispering, scratching noise. Feeling like she was in a dream, Mirren crept to the window. She opened the curtains to the still darkness of the night.

A single white feather was floating on the other side of the glass, suspended in the air, twirling, its hollow shaft gently scratching at the glass.

At first Mirren did nothing but stare at the feather, watching it catch the cold glow of the streetlamps. Then she remembered the phone in her hand.

"Who are you?" she asked.

"My name is Daniel Holmes," came the voice through the hiss of static.

"Am I dreaming, Daniel Holmes?"

"No, Mirren."

"So what you said about my mum… about her being in trouble…"

"It's true, Mirren. She needs your help. *We* need your help."

Mirren's throat was tight. "Who is this 'we'?"

"My shop, Mirren. The Nowhere Emporium. And everyone in it. It's a place filled with brilliant magic, but that magic can be dangerous in the wrong hands."

"But what does this have to do with my mum? With me?"

"Your mum is…" The line hissed and whistled. "… trapped inside the shop…" A moment of silent terror. "He's almost here. He knows where I am. Please, Mirren, come to the Nowhere Emporium! Find your mum. Follow the feather. And trust the sign of the book. Please hur—"

The line went dead.

"Hello?" Mirren shook the phone, as if that would help. "Hello? Come back!"

No answer. Mirren ended the call, let her hand drop, the phone forgotten as she stared through the window at the white feather.

A thought suddenly cut through the dense fog of confusion in her head.

Mum is in trouble. Mum needs my help.

Mirren's head suddenly became very clear. She grabbed her coat and threw it on over her pyjamas, then slipped on a warm pair of socks and her trainers and hurried out to the hall. She picked up her keys and headed for the door, then halted. If this was a wild goose chase, if she was going out into the night in answer to some prank call, Mum might get home before her and find the house empty. She didn't want her to worry, so she wrote a quick note on the chalkboard in the kitchen:

Mum,
Don't worry. I thought you were missing — I've gone to look for you in a shop called the Nowhere Emporium. Be back soon. I'll explain then.
Love you,
Mirren xxx

Satisfied, she hurried out of the flat, locked the door and took the stairs three at a time until she was out in the freezing November darkness. The street was deserted and silent, the air sharp and biting. A thin frost was forming on the pavement. She looked up towards her bedroom window and saw the white feather still scratching at the windowpane.

"Hey," she whispered, feeling foolish for speaking to a feather. "I'm down here."

It was as if the feather had heard her. It spun around, hung in the air for a moment, and then came tearing down towards her. She ducked as it flew over her head, around her in tight circles, and then headed off up the street.

"Wait. Wait!"

Mirren took off after it, buttoning her coat as she ran along the street for a hundred metres, and there she found the feather floating serenely in the pale electric streetlamp. She edged closer. It hovered at about head height, and she reached out to touch it. Her fingers had only brushed the feather when it spun away from her, but she had felt its icy cold. The feather drifted to the door of a nearby shop, and it was then that Mirren became truly aware of her surroundings. She was standing, of course, on the pavement in the High Street, outside the newsagents and the butcher. Only…

Only now there was another shop, a shop she'd never seen before, impossibly sandwiched between the two familiar stores.

Her mouth hung open a little as she looked at the dusty window, and the arched doorway, and the sparkling black bricks. Then she looked up further still and read the faded golden sign.

"The Nowhere Emporium," she whispered. The feather was still hanging back, a few paces behind her. "Am I meant to go in?" She laughed at herself.

"I'm talking to a feather!" Then she turned and looked at the shop again, and as her gaze slid over the smooth, twinkling bricks a curious shiver passed through her body. She took another step, and one more, to the door, and reached for the handle—

Hurried footsteps echoed up the street, and Mirren stepped back, peering into the night, hoping that it might be Mum.

She was quite astonished, instead, to see someone else.

There, rushing towards her, was Robyn Prince. She was wearing a fluffy, oversized pink dressing gown and a hideous pair of slippers adorned with countless sequins and plastic jewels. Gobsmacked though she was to see Robyn Prince out in the middle of the night in her pyjamas, Mirren was even more amazed to see that Robyn too was following a feather, this one a shimmering gold.

When Robyn's feather reached Mirren's, Robyn stopped and, panting, seemed to notice Mirren for the first time. At once she straightened up and fixed her long, luxurious ribbons of hair. She gave Mirren a cold, incredulous look.

"What are *you* doing here?"

Mirren did not quite know what to say. "I was going to ask you the same thing."

"If you must know," said Robyn, "I was… well, I was following that feather."

"Me too." Mirren indicated her own.

Robyn's eyes slid from feather to feather, and then to Mirren. "You mean you've got one too? *You?*"

It was quite amazing to Mirren that, worried though she was about her mum, Robyn could still find a way to get under her skin. Why wouldn't she, Mirren, have a feather? But before she could say anything, another set of footsteps came echoing up the street, this time from the opposite direction, growing louder and louder. Until Luke appeared, jogging towards them, following a third feather, this one deepest red. The three feathers came together, floating around each other as if in greeting, while the three children stood staring at each other in the middle of the cold autumn night.

"Mirren?" Luke's eyes were wide, and he was hugging himself from the cold, his too-short pyjamas exposing his bare ankles to the frosty air. "What are you doing here?" He looked at Robyn and hugged himself tighter. "What's *she* doing here?"

"Is this some kind of trick?" Robyn folded her arms, fixed Mirren and Luke with a suspicious glare. "Have you two lured me out here to embarrass me and capture it on video or something?"

"Oh, yeah," snapped Luke. "Because we just happened to have a couple of magic feathers lying around and thought we'd waste them on you."

Robyn shot him a dagger of a look.

"Stop it, you two." Mirren's thoughts had turned back to her mum again. "Whatever weirdness is going on, it's brought me here because my mum is in danger."

Luke's eyebrows shot upwards. "Your mum? How d'you know that?"

Mirren brought her mobile out of the pocket of her coat. "I got a call. A really weird one."

"You mean that old thing actually works?" said Robyn, sneering at the phone. She shut up when she saw the look on Mirren's face.

"Anyway," Mirren went on, "someone called Daniel Holmes phoned me. He told me that my mum is in trouble and said I should come here, that I should follow the feather. It was outside my window waiting, like I'd already agreed to come. This Daniel guy says that some creep is holding Mum prisoner in this shop…"

Luke was staring at her as if she'd grown another nose. "I got a message too. Not on my phone, though. I woke up to a strange sound coming from the window, like someone breathing. When I opened the curtain, the window was all fogged up with breath, and someone… *something* was writing a message in it for me."

"What did it say?" The question had come from Robyn, who, in spite of herself, it seemed, was interested.

Mirren could see Luke's face flush in the cold light of the streetlamp. "It said… well, it said Mirren was in trouble, that she needed my help and I should follow the feather." He gave Mirren a glance, and she felt such warmth and love for him that she wanted to hug him, but not in front of Robyn.

"How 'bout you?" she said, turning to Robyn, who seemed all of a sudden to become quite flustered.

"It doesn't really matter, does it? I'm here, aren't I?"

"But surely you got a message too?" said Luke. "Why else would you be here? What did it say?"

"Nothing." She glared at him. "Just drop it, will you?"

They did drop it, because at that moment the door to the Nowhere Emporium swung very slowly open, an intoxicating perfume of bonfires and books and hot cocoa drifting out to greet them. From the darkness of the shop came a sound: something small and metallic dropping to the floor, and rolling.

Sure enough, a tiny, glinting object rolled out onto the street and stopped between their feet. Luke reached down and picked it up.

"It's a compass, I think." He frowned. "But there are no markings on it. Just a dial." When he uttered those words, the dial of the compass in his hand glowed bright silver-blue, like the moon, and spun around to point at the shop entrance. "I think it wants us to go in."

"You don't have to come," said Mirren, trying to sound brave. "I'll go in alone. It's my mum who's missing. It might be dangerous, and I wouldn't want anything to happen to either of you."

"Oh, stop trying to be a hero," said Robyn, rolling her eyes. She pushed past them, walked to the door and stopped at the threshold. Reaching out, she touched the sparkling black brick, withdrew her hand. "It's like ice." Then, with a quick look back at them, she disappeared into the darkness beyond.

"Whatever's in there," said Luke, staring after Robyn, "I'd be shocked if it's any scarier than her."

Mirren laughed. "I suppose we'd better go after her."

And with that, they edged towards the door, shoulder to shoulder, and stepped into the Nowhere Emporium.

CHAPTER 7
THE GIRL

Glasgow, December 1990

Daniel Holmes, proprietor of the Nowhere Emporium, stood in the doorway of his shop, breathed in a deep lungful of wintry Glasgow air and smiled. Daniel had been all around the world, first as apprentice to the original owner of the shop, Mr Lucien Silver, and then, when Silver had passed the shop to him, it had been up to Daniel to decide where to go and when, and boy had he seen a lot. From wartime London to ancient Rome, the baking heat of the Old West to the vast snow plains of Canada.

Every stop on the journey, there had been adventure and magic and new people to meet. And yet, as much as Daniel loved the travel, loved the unpredictability of his life, it was always such a thrill to come home. It felt, he thought, like Glasgow fed his soul, that the energy of the city, the smell of the fish and chip shops, the call of the newspaper sellers, recharged him like a battery. And, oh, how he needed recharging. The effort of running the Emporium had continued to strip him of energy, and he was only writing new Wonders in the book sporadically. Thankfully, there had not been another incident like the one in Dubrovnik, when the magic of the book seemed to malfunction.

This trip, he'd parked the Emporium on a side street near the electric bustle of Buchanan Street in December, where shoppers packed the wide boulevard under the twinkling warmth of Christmas lights and window displays. The side street was relatively quiet, home to a few smaller establishments: a pub, a joke shop, a newsagents and a café, from which Daniel had bought the roll and square sausage and cup of hot chocolate he was enjoying now. It was early evening; the sky was black, the air was bitingly cold, and soon Daniel retreated back into the cosy warmth of the dusty old shop, sat down at his desk, and brought the *Book of Wonders* out from a locked drawer.

It was a thick book, bound in shining black leather. When Daniel placed it down upon the desk, five shining gold words on the cover glistened:

The Wonders of
Daniel Holmes

Daniel opened the book to an empty page and brought a fine fountain pen from the pocket of his suit jacket. Being back in Glasgow at Christmastime had sparked an idea in his mind, and it had been several weeks since his last entry. With a little nervousness, he touched the nib of the pen to the thick paper and began to write.

"What are you doing?"

So unexpected was the voice that Daniel's hand jerked across the paper, leaving a trail of black ink. He looked up, saw a young girl standing five or six paces away from the desk. She was small and skinny, lost in a grey-blue padded coat that was far too big. Her hair was auburn, her eyes green and shining with inquisitive wonder.

"Hello," said Daniel, screwing the lid on the pen. "When did you come in?"

"Just now," said the girl.

Daniel squinted at her. "What age are you?"

"Nine. How old are you?"

"That's a wee bit complicated," Daniel replied, waving the question away. "Are you here all by yourself?"

"Nope. Grandad's outside, see?" She nodded to the window, and through the dust and grime Daniel saw the outline of a tall man smoking a cigarette. "I told him to wait outside. He was quite pleased. It means he can sneak a smoke. Gran gives him trouble if he smokes too much."

"Good for her," said Daniel. "Does your grandad always do what you tell him to?"

The girl nodded in an agreeable fashion. "Uh-huh. He's a softy." She took a couple of steps closer to the desk, glanced around in conspiratorial fashion. When she spoke, her voice was low. "You want to know a secret?"

Daniel sat forward in his chair. "OK."

The girl looked around, then cupped her hand to her mouth and whispered, "I can do magic."

Daniel's mouth curled upwards into a smile. "Oh, really?"

"Uh-huh. You want to see?"

"Very much," said Daniel. He watched, amused and intrigued, as the small girl looked around the nearby cabinets and shelves. Then her eye settled upon Daniel's desk. A look of great concentration took hold of her features. The sound of soft fluttering made Daniel look down, and what he saw caused him to gasp. The book – Daniel's *Book of Wonders* – had opened upon the desk, and the pages were fanning open and closed, back and forth, blowing Daniel's messy ginger fringe out of his eyes. He slammed his hand down upon the book.

The young girl took a sharp breath. "Have I done something wrong?" Her face was so filled with innocence and sorrow that he felt quite terrible.

"No, of course not! It's just that this book…" He closed the *Book of Wonders* and locked it away in its drawer once more. "It's very important to me." He gave her what he hoped was a reassuring smile. "Tell me, can anyone else in your family do magic? Your grandad maybe?" He pointed to the window, where the tall figure still stood smoking out in the street.

The little girl giggled. "Nope. None of them. And they've told me not to tell anyone. I'm supposed to keep it a secret, or else people might think there's something wrong with me and take me away."

Daniel shook his head. His mind was racing; he kept thinking back to the first time he'd ever come to the Emporium, when he'd met Lucien Silver. The day his new life had begun. "There's nothing wrong with you," he said, jumping up. "Don't let them tell you otherwise. What's your name?"

"Susie. Susie Anderson."

"That's a great name." Susie beamed at him. "You want to see something really cool, Susie?"

"OK."

"Come with me." He led her to the back of the Emporium, to the red velvet curtain, stopping just at the threshold. "You ready?"

Susie nodded.

They stepped through.

At once the dusty, fire-lit gloom of the shopfront was replaced by a wide-open twilight sky, brushed with gold and purple and burning scarlet. The sun was low to the west, and a full moon hung high above, surrounded by a dappling of bright stars. The shopfront had been filled with the sound of ticking clocks, but here the soundtrack was one of carnival music and the breeze in the trees. A city of striped tents stretched out before them, far as the eye could see. Susie breathed deeply, inhaling the smells of cooking hotdogs and toffee apples and popcorn. Her eyes were as wide as the full moon.

"It's my carnival," said Daniel. "Do you like it?"

Susie nodded. "What's in the tents?"

Daniel laughed. It never ceased to amaze him how readily small children would accept the magic. Adults, teenagers – even older children – would often question how it worked. But not kids like Susie. For them, magic was real before they stepped into the shop. The Nowhere Emporium was only confirmation of what they already believed.

"That's for next time," said Daniel.

"Next time?" She looked crestfallen.

"Your grandad's waiting, remember? We can't have him worrying about you."

"But—"

"Come on," said Daniel.

He led her back through the curtain, and the brilliance of the carnival gave way once more to the dim old cave of antiquities. At the front door, they stopped.

"So I can come back?" she asked.

"That's up to you."

"Promise?"

Daniel nodded.

She smiled. "As soon as I saw this place, I knew I was supposed to come in. I just knew it!"

"Run along now," said Daniel. He opened the door for her, and she gave him another smile as she skipped out into the cold Glasgow evening. He left the door open a crack, just enough that he could watch her walking away, hand in hand with her grandfather. His heart was beating very quickly because he knew that this was a decisive moment.

For three years, he had been on his own, travelling the world, looking for someone with whom he could share the Nowhere Emporium's secrets. But, until now, he hadn't managed to find anyone suitable for the task. Could it be possible that the very person he longed to find had just come to him, had walked through the shop door without knowing why, as he, Daniel, had done years earlier?

He watched Susie grow smaller, felt his hope shrink with her every step.

If she was not meant to return, she would not

remember the shop or meeting Daniel; for that was part of the enchantment surrounding the Nowhere Emporium, protecting it. Nobody from the everyday world ever came back for a second visit.

Long ago, Daniel had been the first return customer. Would Susie be the second?

He watched her approach the street corner.

And then she stopped and looked back.

She smiled and waved.

Daniel's breath caught in his throat. Half in a dream, he opened the door fully and returned her wave.

Then she was gone.

Two days later...

"Susie! Don't go too far ahead now!"

Susie wasn't listening to her grandad. Such was her excitement to see the Nowhere Emporium again, she dashed ahead of him, out of Buchanan Street and into the quiet, narrow road where she'd found the shop. Two days had gone by since her first visit, but it seemed like two weeks. The place was stuck in her head, filling her every thought, every dream.

Running now, her footsteps echoed up the street until she came to a sudden stop, her green eyes staring out in confusion from beneath a furry winter hat.

"Where…"

She looked up and down the street, not noticing the flurry of light snow that had begun to fall. She was staring at the spot where she'd found the shop; she knew this to be true. And yet…

The Nowhere Emporium was gone.

Disappointment crashed around her insides. She felt hurt and foolish and betrayed. He had promised her, the older boy in the shop, that she could come back, hadn't he? Why had he lied?

"Susie!" Grandad's hands on her shoulders brought her back for a moment, but soon she was gone again, not hearing the lecture he was giving her about running off by herself. She wondered if she might have dreamed the shop.

No. It had been real.

It was still real, and she would find it again.

She took Grandad's hand and, much to his puzzlement, began to lead him away. As she went, she could not know that Daniel Holmes was watching, overjoyed that she had come back, feeling, for the first time in years, that he was not alone in the world.

CHAPTER 8

THROUGH THE CURTAIN

The Nowhere Emporium, Present Day

"I don't understand. It's just a shop. A weird shop, I'll give you that, but a shop all the same. Why would we possibly need a compass to get to the centre?" It seemed Robyn was quite right: the Nowhere Emporium, while impressively dark and mysterious and crammed with a singularly random collection of odds and ends, trinkets and treasures, seemed nothing more than a shop. "I mean, look at this!" She held up a stuffed seagull, sending a plume of dust into the air. "Who in their right mind would have something like this in their house? No wonder it's covered in dust. I bet I'm the first person to touch it in years."

Mirren was standing by a grand fireplace nearby, looking up at the walls, which were covered in a great many clocks and mirrors. In one of those mirrors she saw the compass in Luke's hand suddenly flare bright, and she spun to face him.

"It wants us to go this way, I think." He was pointing off towards the shadows at the back of the shop. When he walked away, such was the thickness of the gloom that Mirren almost lost sight of him among the myriad small, gleaming things scattered on shelves and in cabinets. "There's a curtain back here," he called. "I think there's something behind it!"

Mirren moved towards his voice, almost tripping when her foot caught on a length of silken scarf. She found him standing at the curtain; it was deepest red, and it rippled slightly, caught in a breath of cool air from whatever lay beyond. Luke held out the compass so that she could see the glowing dial pointing resolutely forward.

"It's probably just a storeroom, right?" he said. His voice was shaky.

Mirren met his gaze. "Right."

Luke reached for the curtain, but Mirren stopped him. "Wait! We should all go through together, don't you think? I mean, Daniel Holmes called us all here together, didn't he? Whoever he is."

Luke nodded. "I think you're right. This is so messed up, isn't it?"

"Hey, Robyn?" called Mirren.

Robyn had found a stuffed stoat and, it seemed, was having a staring competition with it. She looked over at them. "What?"

"The compass seems to be telling us to go through this curtain."

She gave a sigh and made her way through the maze of display cabinets and columns of books. When she reached them, she stood, hands on hips, and examined the curtain. Then she nodded at the compass. "How come he gets to hold it?"

Mirren gave her a sideways glance. "*What?*"

"The compass. How come Puke is the one holding it?"

A bubble of anger formed in Mirren's stomach. "His name is Luke. Or Lukasz."

Robyn flicked back a lock of hair. "Pfft. Fine. How come *Luke* gets to be in charge of the compass? Why can't I hold it?"

"I don't really mind," said Luke. "Honestly, she can have—"

"No!" Mirren stood tall. "No, she cannot."

"Oh!" said Robyn. "I suppose *you* want it then! How's that going to work if you've only got—"

"What?" said Mirren. "Only got one arm?"

Robyn looked a little sheepish. "I just meant… one free hand. You know."

There was a scandalised expression on Luke's face.

"She can do anything as well as you, Robyn. Better in fact!"

"It's OK, Luke." Mirren looked at Robyn and familiar frustration boiled up inside her. People sometimes doubted her, told her that she could not do things, and there were occasions when she'd felt like screaming. Then, years ago, she'd decided that the best way to live her life was not to argue or waste energy on anger but show the doubters that she was capable. She would show Robyn. "I don't want the compass. Luke has it because he was brave enough to pick it up. And I think he's meant to have it anyway. I've got a feeling..."

"What are you going on about?" said Robyn, looking at Mirren as if she was speaking another language. "You got psychic powers now?"

Mirren took a deep breath, tried to calm herself. "Robyn, of all the people to be stuck with tonight, *believe* me, you'd be the last I'd choose. But here we are. I'm starting to think that my mum is in real trouble, and for whatever reason, this shop has brought the three of us here. Now, me and Luke are going through that curtain, and when we do, Luke is going to be the one reading the compass. Are you coming or not?"

Robyn's watery blue eyes shifted from Mirren to Luke, and then to the curtain. She pulled the golden feather from her pocket, and the edges of it caught a little of the cold light from the compass hand. It seemed an argument was happening inside her head. "Fine," she said, still looking at the feather. "I'll come."

Mirren nodded. "Right then. Let's go."

It seemed to dawn on the three of them at once that, now they had agreed a course of action, they would have to actually go through the curtain. They stood close together, staring at the red velvet for quite a while.

"Who should go first?" said Luke, his voice almost a whisper.

"Together," said Mirren. "We'll go together."

"On three?" Robyn sounded breathless.

"Yeah. Ready?" Nobody answered.

Mirren decided to count anyway. "One... two... three..."

CHAPTER 9
TREASURE AND TROUBLE

The Nowhere Emporium, Present Day

When the curtain fell away, they stood in awed silence, their eyes bugging out of their sockets, their mouths hanging loose.

"This isn't real," said Luke. "This can't be real."

Only the thickness of the curtain fabric separated them from the old shop, and yet it seemed like they had travelled to another world. The dim shopfront had given way to a dazzling, cavernous throne room. They stood in the central chamber, countless floors reaching up into darkness high above, framed with shining golden bannisters and railings. The entire place was crammed with high dunes of gold coins and precious stones, with shining, jewel-encrusted Fabergé eggs and vases taller than any person.

Mirren reached down, picked up a coin. It was heavy and solid, and she placed it between her teeth and bit down, the cold taste of gold filling her mouth. She had seen people do this in movies. "Feels real."

"We're rich!" Robyn was wandering around with a mad, greedy smile plastered across her face, her eyes reflecting the bright glow of the surrounding treasure. She picked up a ruby the size of a duck egg and made to slip it into her dressing gown pocket.

"Wait!" Mirren yelled.

"Blimey, Mir!" Luke pressed his hand to his chest. "You nearly killed me!"

"What's up with you?" said Robyn, her face screwed up.

Mirren shook her head. "I don't think we should take anything." A feeling of dread was creeping up her throat. She tossed the coin back to the floor with a loud clink. "Please. I just want my mum back."

Robyn scowled, but she begrudgingly put the huge ruby back on the pile.

"What's the compass saying?" Mirren asked.

Like the others, Luke had been staring around in wonder at the sudden change in surroundings. Reminded about the compass, he gave it a long look, and frowned. "That's weird. The hand has gone crazy. Look."

Mirren and Robyn came closer and saw that the glowing dial of the compass was spinning around, first in one direction, then the other, fast and slow, seemingly without rhyme or reason.

"So what are we supposed to do now?" said Robyn.

From the corner of her eye, Mirren thought she saw a flicker of movement, and she looked across the room to where a huge throne sat beneath an immense stained-glass window. The window captured her attention. She looked up and up, taking in the details. The window depicted a man in a suit holding a book, an adoring crowd bowing before him. The more she studied it, the more troubled she became. Were the people bowing? Or were they cowering in fear? Their faces…

She snapped her gaze down to the throne, was sure she caught a glimpse of something there, a shadow…

"Hello? Is someone in here with us? Mum? Mum, is that you?" Mirren edged forwards, her feet slipping here and there on piles of coins, every step taking her nearer the throne. As she approached, it struck her how huge it was. She tried to imagine who – or what – might sit in a seat that enormous.

The air near the throne grew chill, and when Mirren reached out and touched the stone seat, it was so cold that her fingers stuck to it and she had to peel them away. In her pocket, she felt the white feather tremble and grow hot.

A sudden, howling rush of air swept through the throne room, followed by a deep, low rumble. Mirren and Luke spun around and saw Robyn standing on a pile of gold. The colour had drained from her face; she looked terrified. "I-I think I've messed up…" she said shakily.

Mirren took a few paces towards her. "Robyn, what did you do?"

Robyn stared back at her with wide eyes. She reached into her pocket, brought her hand back out and opened her fist. In her palm sat the duck-egg-sized ruby.

"Robyn! I asked you not to take anything!"

The rumbling grew louder.

"I didn't think anyone would miss one wee ruby!"

Mirren rushed towards Robyn, stopped just shy of her, and pushed up onto her tiptoes so they were eye to eye. "I swear, if this puts my mum in any danger…"

"Mir!" Luke's shout sounded panicked.

"What now?" She looked back, and horror flooded her body. A great pile of treasure had begun to tremble and move, the coins and jewels and strings of pearls tangling and merging together. The treasure pile rose up, grew arms and legs and a misshapen head. Candlestick horns erupted from the head, and the eyes were fist-sized emeralds that emitted a sickly green glow. The monster – that's what it was: a monster made of treasure – seemed all at once to realise that it was alive, and that it had a duty.

The head swung around, throwing off coins in a glittering shower, and the eyes found Mirren and Robyn. A hole emerged in the face, and from its depths came a bellowing metallic roar.

Mirren heard a scream beside her, and then Robyn barged past and began running towards the curtain back to the shop. But the monster, which looked lumbering and slow, moved deceptively quickly across the ground, and in three earth-shaking strides had cut off Robyn's path. She tried to stop, but the loose coins underfoot made her skid and fall, and she landed only a few metres from the beast. It drew up its foot and Robyn rolled out of the way as it stamped down with a crash that shook the room, sending a flurry of gold flying in all directions.

Mirren grabbed Robyn by the arm, guided her towards Luke.

"What do we do?" he yelled.

"I'm sorry!" Robyn screeched. "I didn't mean it!"

"It's a bit late for that!" said Mirren. "It's coming back!"

The treasure beast had reformed, its shattered foot made new from the surrounding treasure.

"Behind here," said Mirren, pulling them away to crouch in the shadow of the giant throne.

They hardly dared draw breath as they peered out; the treasure beast was walking slowly around, each step a thundering crash, all the while raining loose coins and jewels and gathering more. Its candlestick-horned head swung this way and that, cold emerald eyes searching.

"We need to get out of here," whispered Luke.

"Oh, good thinking!" hissed Robyn. "That hadn't occurred to me, you idiot!"

"*I'm* the idiot?" Luke's face twisted in indignation. "You're the one who nicked a jewel and made that… whatever it is appear!"

"Will you shut it, both of you!" Mirren had been watching the creature with interest. "I think it's moving in a pattern."

"A what?" said Robyn.

"A pattern. Like an end-of-level boss in a video game."

"I," sneered Robyn, "do *not* play video games."

"Well, maybe you should!" said Luke.

Mirren was losing patience, fast. "In video games, at the end of each level, there's often a boss you have to beat to get to the next one. Usually, bosses move in a pattern, so you can watch and learn how to avoid them or take your chance to strike."

"Strike?" Robyn looked aghast. "You want to fight this thing?"

"Of course not! I want to get away from it. Look, it's moving in a certain way, just like I said. See how it's going right around the outside of the hall, checking behind each column?"

"You're right!" said Luke.

"If we move quick, while it's still all the way over there and distracted, we can hide behind columns and piles of treasure, make a dash for the curtain and then come up with a new plan once we're safe."

"I don't like this," said Robyn.

"That's weird," quipped Luke. "I'm having the time of my life."

"Enough, you two!" Mirren was watching the treasure monster again. It was just reaching a marble column on the far side of the hall. "We don't have any other choice. We've got to go. Now!"

They made a move, creeping as quickly and as quietly as they could manage from behind the throne to the nearest column, ducking behind it. Breathless, Mirren peeked out and saw the treasure beast lumbering to the next column all the way across the throne room. She gave the signal and led the others to the safety of the next hiding spot, behind a mound of golden coins. They followed the same pattern, again and again, until they were only a few moves away from a final dash to the curtain.

They were halfway between hiding places when the plan went wrong.

As he moved, Luke's elbow caught on a hanging string of pearls and his weight pulled on the necklace, which in turn dislodged a grand-looking silver plate, sending it crashing and clanging to the floor.

They froze in place.

Across the vast throne room, the treasure monster's head shot up. It swung around and captured them in its cold green gaze. That dark cave of a mouth opened once more, spewing out coins, sending a deafening metallic roar reverberating all around the hall.

"Leg it!" yelled Mirren.

Robyn took off first, leaving Mirren and Luke in her wake. Mirren's foot slipped on the loose coins underfoot and she almost went down, but Luke grabbed her arm and helped her stay upright. Another roar, and a series of thunderous footsteps told them the monster was on the move. Mirren glanced across the throne room, saw the beast clattering towards them, leaping treasure dunes. But the curtain was close, close enough that they could make it...

A flash of gold. Something massive flew overhead at great speed. Mirren looked up in time to see the treasure beast exploding into the wall above the curtain. The throne room shook. Where the beast had been, there was a rain of jewels and coins, and of masonry and brickwork. The wall crumbled, sending Mirren and her companions diving for cover.

Silence and stillness.

Mirren lay on the ground for a moment, listening to her heartbeat thundering in her ears, amazed and grateful that it was still beating. "Is everyone OK?" she whispered, scrambling up.

"Fine!" said Luke.

"I'm not hurt if that's what you mean," moaned Robyn. "But I'm definitely not OK. Look at this!"

The dust was clearing, and as Mirren approached Robyn her heart sank. The beast had thrown itself into the wall on purpose, and now the curtain was completely blocked by huge chunks of marble and twisted golden railing.

"Um, Mir?" Luke's voice was quivering. "I think we better get outta here. Now."

Coins were moving again, rolling and gathering into a seething mass. The beast was reforming.

Mirren scouted around, desperate, frightened. Above, countless galleried hallways lined with doors stretched up forever into darkness. "Any joy with the compass?"

Luke held out the instrument – the dial was flicking back and forth lazily, with no sense of purpose.

Nearby, the treasure beast had almost fully reformed; its emerald eyes glowed, fixed on the intruders. It gave a coughing roar and took a staggering, faltering step.

"We'll just have to take our chances!" said Mirren. "C'mon!"

Away they ran, leaving the central chamber and up a grand staircase to the next floor, where they followed the glittering golden railing, the gallery affording them a bird's-eye view of the treasure-laden throne room below. A movement across the hall caught Mirren's eye, and she saw, unmistakeably, the shadowy outline of a gigantic figure sitting on the throne. It was only a glimpse, for a few seconds at most, and then it flickered and was gone. This strange sight coincided with a short burst of high-pitched humming that screamed out of the compass; the dial spun around so quickly that it began to smoke. Then a deep, echoing laugh filled the throne room, followed by the sound of many clicking locks and chains.

Click.

Click.

Click-clunk-click…

The sound reverberated all around them, from every direction. Robyn lunged forward, grabbed the handle of the nearest jewel-encrusted door. "It's locked." Panicking, she tried the next, and the next. "They all are."

The floor ahead exploded.

Up through the carnage came the treasure beast. There it stood, blocking the way, larger than before, coins dripping from its gargantuan body.

It came lumbering towards Mirren. She was frozen to the spot, unable to move as the glittering beast came nearer, and nearer, and reared back…

It roared.

Then it charged.

A hand on Mirren's shoulder spun her around, and she found herself looking into Robyn's frightened face.

"Run, you idiot. Come on!"

They whirled away, felt the wind from the creature's swiping arm as it narrowly missed them. Then they were sprinting as fast as they could without direction or any semblance of a plan, sure that they would soon meet their end as the treasure monster rumbled after them.

They darted to the left, down a passage leading away from the throne room. The palace hallway was grand, all splashed with gold. Their feet sunk into a luxurious red carpet, and the walls were lined on either side with many paintings in grand frames and bejewelled doors with shining nameplates. Another great rumble came tearing through the passage, and they looked back to see the treasure beast following, struggling to fit through the hallway, scraping at the walls and doors as it tore forward, ripping at the ceiling with its candlestick horns.

"It's gaining!" yelled Luke.

"I want to go home!" cried Robyn.

What happened next happened very quickly indeed.

Ten metres ahead, the air shimmered. Then, after a blinding spark of light, a doorway appeared in the centre of the hallway. The door flew open and a flood of cold daylight spilled into the passage, a chill breeze breathing out of the room beyond, carrying crystals of fresh snow.

"Look there!" called Mirren. "A way out!"

The treasure beast screamed, redoubled its efforts, and started to close the gap.

Five metres…

Four…

Three…

Mirren's legs burned, but she urged her exhausted muscles to carry her faster, faster, faster, until, with a final leap, she was through the door.

She landed on a freezing, soft cushion of fresh snow, heard the muffled thumps of Luke and Robyn crashing down nearby. Scrambling up, she saw the doorway in the snow, stared back into the corridor they'd come from at the monster only a few metres away, its glowing green eyes locked on her.

Mirren screamed, slammed the door shut. The doorway exploded in a shower of twinkling silver smoke and was gone. Mirren stared at the spot where the door had been, her mouth open. "What the…"

"You OK, Mir?" Luke picked himself up and dusted snow from his pyjamas. He pointed to the empty space next to Mirren where the doorway had been. "How did you make that doorway disappear?"

"I don't know. I just shut the door."

"My slippers!" Robyn moaned. "Look at my slippers. Dad paid a fortune for these. He'll be so mad."

Mirren felt a tap on the elbow, turned to see Luke staring at her, pale and shell-shocked. "Mir, am I seeing things, or are we in… in the woods?"

"You're not seeing things," she told him. "We are in the woods. Which is impossible, seeing as we're still indoors. Right?" She leaned down, picked up a handful of snow. It was cold and soft and melted between her fingertips. The air was crisp, filled with the clean smell of pine trees and winter leaves. Every breath left her in a small silvery coil of mist.

"You'll find out pretty quickly that nothing in this place is impossible."

The voice startled them, but not as much as seeing a figure emerging from among the nearby trees. As he came from the shadows, he held up his hands as if to show that he was not a threat. But Mirren and her companions did not really notice this detail. They could see nothing beyond the shining circles of glowing yellow glass he had for eyes, and the face made of pins and cogs and gears.

The man coming towards them was made entirely of metal.

CHAPTER 10

INFINITUM

Glasgow, May 1992

The morning of Grandad's funeral was bright and sunny, with a sky as sparkling blue as the old man's eyes had been in life.

Susie sat alone in her bedroom on the floor at the foot of her bed, her legs crossed in front of her. Her eyes were focussed on a spot in the air a foot or so above her head, where a red-and-black-striped HB pencil was floating. Susie knew that she was not supposed to be doing this; her parents had pleaded with her to hide her abilities ever since they'd started to show. If anyone found out what she could do, they said, she'd be taken away and experimented upon and probably never see her family or friends again. Susie had always believed this to be true, and she had always tried to obey, even when the temptation to use her powers was great.

This morning, though, she did not care if Mum or Dad came through the door and caught her levitating the pencil. She was angry at them, you see, for not allowing her to attend Grandad's funeral.

"But I want to go!" she'd pleaded. "I want to say goodbye!"

"I'm sorry, Susie Bear," her dad had said. "A funeral isn't the place for children. We'll have our own little thing in the garden later, eh? You can say something if you want."

But Susie could not understand why she was not allowed to go. Grandad had been her friend, her partner in crime since she'd been old enough to walk. He'd taken her to school on those mornings Mum and Dad both had work. He'd come to the shows they could not attend, taught her all about the planets and the stars, sparked her interest in science.

And he had been the only one who had not been frightened of her gift, her abilities. When nobody else was around, he'd encourage her to practise, and he'd laugh as she'd sharpen pencils without touching them or make her dolls walk around the room.

Back in the here and now, hot tears ran down her face; mostly tears of sadness, but also of anger at the world for taking him away so soon. She stared at the pencil floating above her head and blinked. It snapped cleanly in two and fell to the ground.

The sound of a car engine out in the street made her get up and check the window. Her breath caught in her throat. The hearse was outside, long and black and solemn. And there, in the back, was the coffin, surrounded by lilies and a display of little blue flowers that spelled out GRANDAD.

She was breathing heavily now, and she had to wipe the fog of her breath from the window. Panic began to rise in her throat. Surely there had been a mistake? Surely Grandad, always so full of energy and curiosity, could never die? She wanted to run down and throw open the hearse and get him out of that wooden box, wanted to hug him one more time, to smell the strong mints on his breath and see those kind blue eyes. Eyes that, unlike her parents', had always looked into hers without betraying a hint of fear.

A *knock-knock-knock*, and Dad's face appeared around the door. "They're here, Susie Bear," he said. "Your mum and me need to go."

"Please can I come, Dad?"

She could see the pain in his face as he shook his head. "I'm sorry. The family has decided it's best if there are no kids…" He stopped, and closed his eyes tight, and she knew he was pushing tears back. "Your grandad… he loved you very much, you know."

Susie stared at her feet, tears rolling freely, dripping to the floor. Then Dad's fingers were gentle on her chin, turning her face towards his, and she saw he was crying too, saw how much sorrow he was feeling. Because Grandad had been his dad, hadn't he? And he was feeling everything she was. Maybe more. She fell forward and wrapped her arms around him, and they were crying together. They stayed that way until Mum appeared and told them in a gentle voice that it was time to go.

Susie watched the line of cars drive up the street and away, and then she stayed at the window, staring without really seeing, watching the dancing shadows of the trees and the streaks of white cloud speed across the vast blue sky. Watching the sunlight sparkle on the midnight-black bricks of the shop across the road.

What?

Susie blinked. She looked again, rubbed at her eyes to make sure that this was not some kind of mirage. Her heart began to thrum. She spun and burst from her room, took the stairs two at a time and yelled, "Just going out for some air, Mrs Peebles!"

Mrs Peebles, an elderly neighbour who was sitting in with Susie while Mum and Dad were at the funeral, popped her head out of the kitchen and said, "Oh… well don't go too far, dear."

But Susie was already out of the door and down the path and across the street, slowing only when she approached the mysterious, impossible shop between number seventy-two, where the Collins family lived, and seventy-four, where Mr Rickshaw stayed with his yappy little dog.

The Nowhere Emporium, from the outside at least, looked exactly as it had two years previously, when Susie had first come across it in Glasgow city centre. Close enough to touch now, she reached out and brushed the sparkling black bricks with trembling fingers; they were cold as ice. The door was not locked. Susie pushed it open, entered the dim cave of a shop, and stared around once more at the columns of books and birdcages and mirrors, at the stuffed animals and suits of armour and uncountable knick-knacks. All at once it was comforting and terrifying, familiar and strange. The smells, of melting chocolate and bonfires and dusty books, enveloped her.

"Hello again."

And there he was, just as she remembered, the boy in the suit, sitting at his desk as he'd been the night they'd first met.

"You lied to me," she said.

He frowned. His hands were clasped on the desk in front of him. "I did?"

"Yes, you did. You told me I could come back."

He raised an eyebrow. "Yes. And here you are."

"But… but I tried to come back again the next day and you were gone!"

He stood up, put his hands in his pockets. "I said you could come back. I didn't say *when*."

His answer made her hackles rise. "That's a dirty trick and you know it!" She lost her train of thought though, when her eyes found the rich red curtain, and her memories took her back to the carnival beyond.

"I'm sorry about your grandad," said the boy in the suit.

"What? How did you know about that?"

"Well, I've been keeping an eye on you since we last met."

"You have?" said Susie, taken aback. "How come?"

"I think," he said, "maybe we should start again. My name's Daniel. Daniel Holmes." He offered a hand, and she shook it. "I run this place."

"All by yourself?"

"Yes. Well, actually, no. I have a little help. But you'll find that out in time."

"I will?"

Daniel Holmes chuckled. "So, the reason I've been keeping an eye on you from time to time is that... well, you remind me of me. The first time I ever found this shop, I had no clue there was any magic in the world. But the owner of the shop back then saw something in me. He saw potential, and I like to think he was right. Susie, you have so much more potential than I ever did. I could never use magic outside the Emporium the way you can."

Susan could feel her blood pumping through her body. "Really?"

"Really. But you see, when I found the shop, I was in a different situation. I was an orphan. I didn't have a family that loved me like you do. That's why I've kept my distance, see? You have a family, a mum and dad. You have friends. This shop has a way of getting under your skin, of making you forget about other things, and I wouldn't want anything to come between you and your family. So I made a decision to hang back and pay you a visit from time to time, to check in on you, until you're ready."

Susie noticed that Daniel talked with his hands a lot, waving them about as he spoke, to animate his points and drive them home. But now he dropped his hands to his side and looked solemn. "I thought maybe today would be a good day to give you a distraction?"

It was a question more than anything else. Susie suddenly felt a great rush of gratitude. She nodded. "Thanks."

Daniel smiled, spun around and went back to his desk. From a drawer he brought out a book that she recognised at once; Daniel had been writing in it the day they'd first met, and it had haunted her dreams ever since.

"OK." He placed the book on his desk and sat on the deep chair. "Let's see…" He began to flick through the pages, and the more he flicked, the more passages of tightly packed, inky black handwriting Susie glimpsed, the surer she became that there were more pages than ought to be possible. At last Daniel came to a blank page. He sat back, brought a shining fountain pen out from his jacket pocket and tapped the end of it against his chin. "Right. I suppose the best way to do this is to put it plain and simple. Here goes. This book – the *Book of Wonders* – is the key to everything that happens in the Nowhere Emporium. Anything I write down in these pages, Susie, becomes reality somewhere in the shop." He paused, frowned. "At least, that's the idea. Lately, the thing has been misbehaving a bit."

"What do you mean?"

Whatever had been in his head, he shook it away with a wave. "Never mind that. I'm sure it'll work today. Are you ready?"

Susie was eleven years old, standing near the threshold of one of the most important borders in life: the border between childhood and adulthood, between magic and the everyday. When a person crosses this border, when they stop believing, there is usually no way back. The loss of her grandfather had stripped a huge amount of magic from her life. Without him to encourage her, to remind her that she was gifted, she had begun to worry that she would forget, that one day she would wake up and her magic would be gone. Worse than that, she wondered if she would even remember if it had ever been there. Things changed when you grew up, after all.

But here, in this place, it seemed that anything was possible. The magic crackled in the very air she breathed, and when she stared at the blank page of the *Book of Wonders*, her very soul lit up.

"Anything you write comes to life?" she whispered. "Anything at all?"

"Anything," said Daniel. "And I thought maybe we could come up with something in memory of your grandad."

"Just for him?"

"Yeah. Big or small. Fancy or simple. Whatever you want."

Susie's mind whirred and sparked, and soon an idea burned bright as a candle in her mind. "How about something like this…"

It took them a while, because they wanted it to be perfect. When they were done, and Daniel had closed and locked away the book, they pushed through the curtain to the caramel-scented, twilight-dipped carnival and began to weave through the myriad tents and stalls, greeting performers along the way, ducking between the legs of giant elephants and stilt-walkers until, after walking for a very long time, they came to a new tent. It was fashioned from a purple velvet so rich and deep that it seemed to be cut from the sky above. The entrance was buried in folds of that same velvet, and as they pushed through, the sight that greeted them on the other side was more wondrous, more incredible, than even Susie's imagination had allowed.

Grandad's dream had always been to visit a place called the Hayden Planetarium in New York City. He had newspaper clippings and magazines devoted to the great spherical theatre, where images of the night sky were beamed onto a screen over the heads of amazed onlookers. He had never made it there.

The room in which Susie found herself now – the room that she had helped Daniel to write in the pages of the book – was not a planetarium. It was something better.

It was a model of the universe.

No. Not just a model.

It *was* a universe. An entire universe, in a single room.

It felt wonderfully strange to be floating in the depths of space. But in this room, there was no need for a spacesuit or ship. Their ship, Susie knew without question, was their imagination.

When they moved, stars passed in blazing streaks of light. They covered unimaginable distances in moments, visiting foreign solar systems, planets made of diamond, moons spewing vast jets of ice crystals into the darkness of space. They witnessed the birth and death of stars, watched the universe grow and expand and fill with marvels beyond their wildest dreams, until at last they reached more familiar territory, passed planets Susie recognised: Saturn with its wondrous rings, Jupiter with its great red spot, and finally, the most wonderful of all, a blue-and-green marble hanging in the dark.

Earth.

Down and down they came, seeing the continents, down towards the UK, to Scotland, to Glasgow, to Susie's street. And there was the Emporium, across from her house as it had been in the real world. Daniel had been beside her all the way, a journey that might have taken a million years, or five minutes, or a fraction of a second. He gave her a smile, held open the door to this Emporium within an Emporium, and she walked through…

For a moment she felt like she was falling.

Then she was back outside the twilight-purple tent in the Carnival of Wonders, inhaling the scent of caramel and popcorn. "Are we back for real? Is this where we started?" She was breathless and giddy.

"We're back," Daniel said.

Susie could not help it; she leapt forward, grabbed him, this strange boy she hardly knew, and hugged him tight. When she finally let go, she saw that he was embarrassed. "Sorry. I couldn't help it. It's just that…

Grandad would have loved it so much. I can see him flying through the stars, taking it all in."

"Maybe," said Daniel, "somewhere out there, somewhere we don't understand, he is."

"It's time to go, isn't it?" she asked, though she knew the answer.

"Aye. For now."

They walked back to the curtain, and the shopfront, and the door to Susie's familiar world. She found herself crying again, but the burning sting of emptiness had lessened, replaced by a feeling that she was somehow closer to Grandad.

"See you," said Daniel.

Susie smiled, and walked through the door to the bright spring day. She took a few paces, tilting her face up towards the warmth of the sun. When she turned around and saw that there was nothing between house numbers seventy-two and seventy-four, that the Nowhere Emporium was gone, she did not feel sad. She was not at all concerned that she would not see Daniel again, or walk among the carnival tents.

This, she knew, had only been the beginning.

Daniel sat at his desk by the light of the fire, poring over the Universe Wonder he'd just created. Well, that was not strictly true. Susie had created it. She had told him what to write, explaining her imagination with a clarity and precision that he could never hope to match. And the magic in her veins had flowed into the book; he had felt it, felt the connection between Susie and the pages. It was amazing, and curious and, just at the edges of things, slightly troubling. Daniel had not seen such a connection to the *Book of Wonders* since Lucien Silver himself had been alive – and he was beginning to suspect that Susie's link with the book could become stronger even than that. He had never felt such raw power.

He closed the book, sat back in his chair, sipped from a glass of iced lemonade. He had been searching for years to find someone with whom he could share the Emporium's secrets. Why, then, now that he had finally found her, was he not overjoyed? What was troubling him? Was he jealous of the connection she had to the place?

Surely not.

Trying to distract himself, Daniel opened the book again, turned to a blank page and began to write.

As it turned out, Daniel was correct to be troubled. Susie's energy passed through the labyrinthine

Emporium like a shockwave. Everything in the shop felt it: every Wonder, every creature, every performer, in every corner.

And far, far away, in the infinite depths of the place, a dormant darkness stirred.

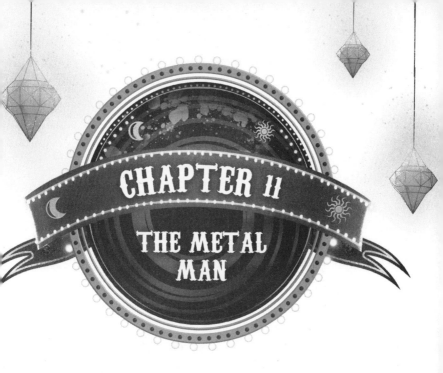

CHAPTER 11
THE METAL MAN

The Nowhere Emporium, Present Day

"Stay back!" Robyn had taken off one of her slippers and was brandishing it at the approaching metal man. "I mean it!"

"It's OK," he said in a deep, clear voice. "I'm a friend."

Robyn snorted. "Yeah? That's exactly what someone who's not a friend would say!"

He was made of gears and springs, and his metal clothes were, it seemed, not the clothes of a lumberjack as one might expect in such woodland surroundings, but of a circus ringmaster. His face was a marvel to behold: a jigsaw of metal cogs and pins that were constantly moving and interlocking and shifting to create the illusion of animated features. He stopped a safe distance away, his hands still held up to show he meant no harm. "How did you get here?" he asked.

"We're not answering your questions, buster," said Robyn, still brandishing her slipper.

"Oh, put that down, Robyn," said Mirren. "What are you hoping to do? Knock him out with the smell?"

Robyn looked scandalised. Her face flushed pink as she held onto a tree trunk for balance and put the slipper back on her foot.

"Did you make that door appear back in the hallway?" Mirren asked the metal man. "Did you save us from that… treasure monster?"

He nodded. "Yes. And now that I've answered your question, will you answer mine? How did you get here?"

"Someone called Daniel Holmes brought us here," replied Mirren. "He said an evil magician is keeping my mum prisoner somewhere in the shop. At first I thought it was all a wind-up but…" She gestured around the place. "Not any more. You have to understand, we don't have a clue what's going on! We're just normal kids. An hour ago, I was in bed! We don't know what this place is, or what we're supposed to do. I only know – *hope* – that my mum is here somewhere." As she spoke, her eyes brimmed with tears. Luke hurried over and gave her a balled-up hanky from his pyjama pocket. She blew her nose.

"My name is Ted," said the metal man. "I assure you, you're safe here for now. I'll do my very best to explain what I can, but first, I ask that you tell me exactly what has happened tonight, step by step."

And so they did, first explaining about the strange messages from Daniel Holmes.

"Your mother," said Ted. "Is her name Susan?"

"Yes!" Mirren replied with surprise. "You've seen her?"

"Not recently. Your mum and Daniel knew each other when she was much younger." Ted paused, gathered his thoughts. "It's probably better that I explain a bit about this place. The Nowhere Emporium began as the invention of a great magician called Lucien Silver. Many, many years ago, Mr Silver invented this magical place and began travelling the world and through time."

Mirren and her friends gazed at each other in awe.

"As Silver's power grew, the man who first taught him magic, Vindictus Sharpe, became jealous. He wanted the Emporium for himself. And so began a chase that lasted for over a century; Sharpe always on the tail of Silver and his shop, Silver always managing to stay a step or two ahead.

"Eventually, Silver's magic began to fade, and he took on an apprentice, Daniel Holmes. Daniel helped Silver defeat Sharpe, and Silver handed the reins of the shop to Daniel. Everyone was supposed to live happily ever after. But that is not how it worked out.

Sharpe had not been vanquished for good, as we hoped. Instead, it seems that what was left of him somehow became a part of the Emporium, and he waited, and grew stronger, his darkness seeping through the place like poison, making Daniel weak. When Sharpe finally made his move, he took control of most of the Emporium.

"But no matter how he tried, Sharpe could not control it all. Pockets of resistance lingered on. A small number of us – perhaps the most loyal to Daniel – have not yet been turned. To show our loyalty, we've marked ourselves with a symbol." He held out his hand. Etched into the metal was the shape of an open book. "This is the sign of the League of the Book. We fight against Sharpe, fight in the name of Daniel Holmes and the Emporium. Wherever you see this symbol, you know you will find friends."

"Daniel told me to look out for that!" said Mirren.

"And me!" said Luke.

"Me too," said Robyn, unimpressed. "Big whoopee."

"So Mum has been here before," said Mirren. She racked her brains, tried to remember any small mention her mum may have made about Daniel Holmes over the years. There was nothing. "But why did this Sharpe guy want her?"

"She has a strong connection with the Emporium," explained Ted. "As strong as I have ever seen. When Sharpe first brought Susan back, Daniel was so angry;

I'd never seen him like that before. I suspect only he can properly answer your questions, but I have not seen much of him since Sharpe took power. He was forced to run. But I fear Sharpe may have caught up with him."

"And you don't know where Sharpe might be keeping Mum?"

"We think in a place called the Fountain. But Sharpe has hidden it away, deep in the Emporium. We searched and searched for a long time, but all for nothing. And all the while Sharpe grew more powerful."

"Hold on," said Mirren with a frown. "You're talking like Mum's been here for ages. She's only been gone a few hours."

Ted paused. The pins and cogs of his face formed an expression of sympathy. "This will be difficult to understand. From your point of view, your mother has been gone less than a day, yes?"

Mirren nodded. "That's right."

"But for us… for your mother… it has been much longer. Time has different qualities in the Emporium, you see."

Mirren took a step towards him, a terrible sickness rising in her throat. "So how long has she been here?"

Ted's glowing glass eyes stared into Mirren's. "I'm afraid your mother has been trapped in the Nowhere Emporium for many years."

CHAPTER 12
THE CURSED COG

The Nowhere Emporium, Present Day

For minutes, nobody spoke. Mirren could not speak, could not organise the multitude of thoughts in her head, the panic and fear and puzzlement. Mum had been in this place – this weird shop – for *years?*

"This is a lot to grasp," said Ted kindly. "It will take time to wrap your thoughts around it, I know."

"What does 'many years' even mean?" Mirren asked. "Ten? Twenty? Fifty?"

"I'm not sure. I'm sorry. I only exist inside the shop. My sense of time is different from yours."

"Does that mean," said Robyn, her round face full of interest, "that her mum might be really old now?"

Luke gave her a scolding look. "Robyn! Maybe now isn't the best time for that question."

"No," said Mirren. "No, it's a good question." Robyn looked pleased with herself and nudged Luke in the ribs. "Actually," Mirren went on, "it's what I was going to ask first. If my mum… if she's been in here that long, she *will* be old, won't she?" The thought of this terrified Mirren so much that she could barely speak the words. Not because being old was a bad thing, but because she was frightened that years and years of time with her mum had been stolen from her, and she would never be able to get them back.

Ted's shoulders sagged. "I wish I could tell you that your mother has not grown old, but I just don't know."

Luke stepped forward. "Maybe this can help find her?" He held out his hand. There, nestling in his palm, was the compass. "It rolled out of the shop when we first arrived, and it seemed to want to guide us, but it's been broken since the throne room."

The metal man stroked his chin, and the sound was like a hammer scraping on an anvil. Long tendrils of steam drifted from his mouth, and Mirren realised that he was somehow breathing. She wondered if he had metal lungs in his metal chest.

"May I?" he asked.

Luke nodded, placed the compass in his large metal hand. Ted handled it with care, turning it over, inspecting every part of it. Then he held it to his chest, almost as if he was hugging it. "I can fix this, I think."

"You can?"

"I'm sure of it. Come with me."

They walked and walked, trudging through the deep undergrowth of the woods, a carpet of fallen leaves and snow and mud. It was hard going.

"My dad is going to sue this place into oblivion," said Robyn. "You wait and see. What sort of shop almost kills its customers? Hasn't this Daniel guy heard of health and safety? I wish I'd never come."

"That makes two of us," muttered Luke.

"Shut it, Puke."

Mirren ignored them. She had been quiet for a while, trying to organise her thoughts. At last she'd come to the conclusion that freaking out, while a perfectly justifiable response to the situation, would not help Mum in any way. Instead, she was going to have to focus. She'd approach this seemingly impossible task the way she'd approached all the other challenges in her life. She'd succeed here, just like she'd succeeded when people told her that having a short arm meant she'd never be a great swimmer, never be able to climb, never be able to do a million different things. It was a matter of thinking about things from a different angle, of finding a way to work around the challenge.

"How is all this possible?" she asked Ted, breaking her silence at last. "It's like we're in another world."

"In a way," said Ted, "you are. The Nowhere Emporium isn't a normal place. It is, I think, the most magical place in all the world. But I don't know for certain because I've never been outside the walls of the shop."

"Never?" asked Robyn, her eyebrows halfway up her forehead.

"No. It's like this..." Ted stopped to gather his words. "The owner of the shop – the true owner – created everything you see, including characters like me, who only exist *inside* the shop. If I were to step through the curtain, I'd turn to dried ink dust and scatter with the wind. But I don't need to leave. There are countless rooms, countless Wonders to explore inside the Emporium, all connected by the *Book of Wonders*.

"As you might imagine, though, such a wondrous place, such power, attracts the kind of folks who want it all for themselves. People like Vindictus Sharpe."

They carried on walking until at last the dense woodland thinned to reveal a log cabin perched at the edge of a clifftop and a vast sweeping valley beyond. Ted led them to the cabin and ushered them inside, where there was no chair, or bed, or cooking range.

Mirren supposed that a metal man might not need to sleep, or sit down, or eat. The only piece of furniture was an enormous workbench in the centre of the cabin, packed full of drawers and scattered with a great many tools: saws and planes and files. Hanging from the ceiling on strings were a collection of carved wooden animals in various stages of completion. Mirren looked all about, saw swans and weasels and mice, owls and snakes and even a great bear. The whole place smelled of wood sap and sawdust.

Ted placed the compass on his workbench and fetched a small metal tool from one of the many drawers. With the tool he opened the casing of the compass, revealing the intricate inner workings: shining metal cogs and gears as slender as moonbeams. In the very heart of the compass he found a larger cog, and cautiously eased it out, holding it in his open palm for them to see. Unlike the brilliant metal of the others, this one was black, as if it had been burnt.

"Sharpe's powers have seeped inside," he said. "He must have cursed it somehow. Did you see him in the throne room?"

"No," said Robyn. "We were a bit distracted by the massive gold monster trying to kill us."

"And we know why it came, don't we?" snapped Luke. "If *someone* hadn't been so greedy and tried to steal a ruby, maybe we wouldn't have been in trouble at all!"

"I saw him," said Mirren quietly. The others fell silent. "I saw Sharpe. At least, I think I did. In the throne room. A dark shape sitting on the throne. Didn't you guys hear him laughing when we ran away from the treasure monster?"

Luke and Robyn were staring at her, open-mouthed.

"I didn't hear him, Mir," said Luke.

"Me either," said Robyn.

"Well, he was there. And when he laughed, that's when the compass started to smoke."

Ted was holding the cursed cog as if it were a scrap of diseased flesh or some poisonous insect. "It sounds to me like Sharpe has cursed the compass. Strange that he did not try to intercept you himself."

Mirren remembered the feather in her pocket, how it had grown warm when she had approached the huge throne. She took the white feather out, held it up, brilliant and pure. Ted came closer, reached out. As his iron fingertips touched the feathers, sparks shot off, and he withdrew his hand. The many pins and cogs that made up his face settled into a look of realisation.

"This feather is bursting with powerful enchantments; made by Daniel to protect you from Sharpe, I guess, which explains why he didn't harm you himself and instead sent the treasure monster after you and cursed the compass."

"But you can fix the compass?" asked Luke.

Ted took the cursed cog and placed it carefully on his bench. He then did something that made Mirren and her companions gasp. He took his fingers and, with great ease, and as if it were the most everyday occurrence, opened a door in his belly so that his inner workings were clearly visible: an intricate system of many whirring cogs and spinning gears and pumping pistons, all interlinked and working in perfect harmony. Next, he reached into his belly and, with a shower of bright silver sparks, pulled out one of the cogs.

"Doesn't that hurt?" Robyn grimaced, looking as though she might throw up.

Ted only gave her a sideward glance and proceeded with delicate fingers to click the cog into place inside the compass. At once the dial came to life, glowing brightly and spinning around in a blur before settling resolutely on one direction.

"It's working again!" Luke dashed forward to pick it up, but then withdrew his hand quickly.

"It's alright," said Ted. "It seems you've been chosen as navigator. Please, pick it up."

Luke scooped the compass off the workbench. "It's warm again."

A small, tremulous sound made everyone stop and look at the workbench, where the burnt cog was now vibrating against the surface.

"Erm, is it supposed to do that?" asked Luke.

As Ted watched the cog tremble against the bench, the countless metal gears and pins of his face arranged themselves into a look of concern. "No. No, it's not." He dashed to the small window, looked out towards the woods. "They are coming."

"Who?" A shock of terror surged up Mirren's spine.

"Sharpe's Nightmares. Inky, mindless monsters that hunt down anyone who's against Sharpe."

"I thought you said this place was safe?" said Robyn, her eyes bulging.

Ted pointed a metal finger at the workbench. "The cog. It must have led them here."

"I see them!" Robyn was at the window, and Mirren saw all the colour drain from her face. She joined Robyn, peered out and spotted, among the dense trees, dark inky shadows that moved with a harsh, gurgling whisper. Nightmares.

"What do we do?" said Mirren. "What are we supposed to do?"

Ted rushed across to Luke, placed his large metal hands on his shoulders, gave him a shake. "You must keep the compass safe, you understand? If I am gone, there will be nobody left who can fix it."

Luke nodded, his eyes stretching wide.

"And you," said Ted, this time to Robyn. "I want you to take this." Again, he opened up the door in his belly, revealing the clockwork innards.

This time he brought out a small key, the handle of which was shaped like an open book. "This key opens doors where there are none."

"What?" Robyn took the key. "What does that mean?"

From above came a heavy thud, and then a scratching sound. Everyone in the cabin froze, staring up at the ceiling. Mirren felt the blood in her veins turn cold. There was something on the roof. Whatever it was, it scrambled up and up, and then the sounds it made began to drift down the chimney, wet and gurgling and hissing. A plume of coal dust fell inwards.

Silence.

Then, all at once, a scrambling, tumbling racket.

Something large and dark landed in the hearth, hissing and spitting. It spun around and stood up, and Robyn let out a scream. The Nightmare shared many similarities with a human – it had a head and two arms and legs – but it was made of a dripping, viscous black liquid. Where there should have been a face was nothing, no nose or mouth or eyes, and as it moved, the edges of it seemed to fade for brief moments, like black smoke.

The thing's head swung from side to side. A hole opened in its face, and from the hole came a long black tongue that tasted the air. They caught a glimpse of rows and rows of sharp, serrated teeth.

It lunged forward, towards Mirren and Robyn, with such an explosion of speed that Mirren was taken by surprise. As the thing was about to grab her, Mirren felt someone pull her down to the ground and away from it in the nick of time. She landed with a thud and saw that Robyn had saved her. Staggering back up, she managed to spin away just as Ted seized a huge hammer from his workbench and swung, connecting with the Nightmare and sending a cloud of ash high into the air.

Ted charged to the door, stepped outside, and the Nightmares flooded forward. He swung the hammer time and again, his hand a blur in the frozen air, until all was silent.

But the fight was not over. From the window, Mirren could see that the surrounding woodland was teeming with these dark things, that there was no way out.

"You must get away," said Ted. "I will hold them off."

"But we can't leave you," cried Mirren. "There must be some—"

"Daniel Holmes has brought you here for a reason," Ted cut her off. "You must continue your journey. You must succeed. Please, do as I say. Go! There is another door at the back of the cabin."

"What will you do?"

Ted stood tall, held out a hand, and snapped his metal fingers. The glass circles of his eyes burned for a moment, bright as the sun, and in the cabin Mirren and her companions watched in wonder as the multitude of carved wooden animals came to life — the snakes and bears and birds of prey — and gathered at the door or circled in the air.

Ted gave the children one last look with those burning yellow eyes, bowed, and then turned to face the surrounding Nightmares. He stared out at them for a long, long moment. Slowly, he raised his hand, and snapped his fingers again.

The wooden animals charged.

The Nightmares came to meet them.

The sounds of snapping and hissing and crunching filled the air. Luke ran to the door, bolted it tight.

"There!" said Mirren. "The other door."

The second door led out to the back of the cabin, where they came to a stop at the edge of a great clifftop.

"What now?" asked Luke.

"What does the compass say?"

Luke consulted the instrument. What little colour remained in his face vanished. He pointed out over the cliff edge.

"What?" Robyn shook her head. "No way!"

They moved slowly to the very edge, looking out over an unimaginable drop to the valley below, where a huge river snaked off to the horizon like a silver rope.

One of the Nightmares came crashing through the

back door, fell to the ground, and then, dripping inky liquid onto the snow, came scrabbling towards them, hissing and spitting and grabbing.

"Everything we've seen so far tells us things aren't what they seem here," said Mirren hurriedly. "There's no way this Daniel Homes would lead us off the side of a cliff without there being more to it. I think we have to believe in the compass."

"No!" cried Robyn. "No, I can't, I can't!"

"You can!" Mirren gripped Robyn's arm. "What's the alternative, hmm?"

"Together!" said Luke, moving between them as he put the compass in his pyjama pocket. "Take my hands, both of you."

"Together," repeated Robyn in a whisper.

A black wave of inky creatures came flooding through Ted's cabin, around it, over it.

Standing either side of Luke, Mirren and Robyn each took a hand. Mirren closed her eyes and felt Luke's warm hand in hers. She thought of Mum. Then, as one, they ran forward and leapt off the cliff edge, into the waiting unknown.

CHAPTER 13

BIRTHDAY

Glasgow, 1996

Susie Anderson sat at the dressing table in her bedroom, stared at her reflection and smiled. All in all, her fifteenth birthday had been one to remember. Mum and Dad, taking the many hints she'd dropped on them like anvils over the past few months, had got her the new telescope she'd wanted so much; it sat proudly in the corner of her room now, assembled and ready to use just as soon as the skies cleared, which did not look likely any time soon.

It was Saturday, so there was the added bonus of not having to go to school, of enjoying a lie-in and a day spending her birthday money at the local shopping centre with her friends. And it had been there, in the food court outside the pizza place, that Kevin Feather had asked her to the end-of-term disco.

Just thinking about it now made her face flush and her chest flutter. Kevin Feather! Kevin Feather, who'd once made her furious by being the only person in the year to beat her score in a science test. Kevin Feather who was in the chess club, and played clarinet, and wanted to be an astrophysicist. Kevin Feather, who had that cute Canadian accent and whom she'd had a crush on for months. That Kevin Feather.

She had already begun to imagine what she might wear to the disco. Dad had been teasing her over dinner about having a boyfriend, and she'd laughed and acted outraged, but inside she was flying.

And the day was about to get even better.

She checked her watch. Almost five to midnight. Her stomach was filled with butterflies as she stood up, and went to the window, and looked across the street.

A pang of doubt crept into her head.

He *would* come, wouldn't he? Yes, of course he would. He always came on her birthday. Always at five to midnight. Why should tonight be any different?

The second hand of her watch seemed to have slowed to an agonising crawl. Every second seemed like minutes. And then, at last.

Five to midnight.

She went to the window again, her hand shaking as she reached for the curtain, opened it a fraction and peeked through into the night.

She took a sharp breath; her insides were suddenly dancing with excitement. It felt like every Christmas morning she'd had as a child rolled into one. There, across the street, its black bricks sparkling in the light of the streetlamps, was what she had been waiting for.

She slipped into a warm hoodie and dashed out of her bedroom door. Mum was not at all a night owl and was already in bed asleep. When she reached the foot of the stairs, Susie crept to the living room and found Dad, as expected, asleep on the couch, the football highlights playing on the TV.

Smiling to herself, Susie concentrated deeply on the throw on the back of the couch and watched as it lifted up and unfolded in the air before coming down gently to rest on top of Dad, who gave a dreamy smile and shifted a little in his sleep. Then, after kissing him on the forehead, she turned and left the house, almost running across the street in her eagerness.

Through the shop door, she stopped, looked around and smiled, taking deep breaths of the familiar dusty air. The place never changed. Nothing ever seemed to move. Everything was exactly as she remembered from her last visit, some three months ago, and this was exactly how she liked it.

"Hi, Susie."

He was behind his desk, like always, writing in that wondrous book. She approached slowly, the smile on her lips widening with every step, until at last she reached the desk. When they had first met, he had been a few years older than her, and she had thought him so grown up and impressive. Now, though, because of the way time moved in the Nowhere Emporium, she had caught him up, even overtaken him a little as far as she could see; when he stood up she was taller than he was, and from the look of him he might have been thirteen or fourteen.

"Happy birthday." He stepped out from behind the desk, a little awkwardly she thought, and she rushed forward and hugged him tight.

"It's so good to see you!" She broke the hug and swept around in a circle. "So good to see the old place!"

He nodded. "Had a good day?"

"Yeah, great actually. I got a new telescope, and went to the shopping centre with my mates, and this boy asked…" She flushed. "Never mind that. What are we going to do?"

He gave her a curious look. "Um. Well… I thought this year for your birthday I'd give you something special."

"Oh? Special you say?" She raised her eyebrows, and this time it was his turn to blush a little.

"Yeah. Well, I thought... you've been coming here for years now, right?"

"Yeah."

"And you've learned lots of stuff about how the Emporium works, right?"

"Yeah."

"And you've watched me writing in the *Book of Wonders* loads, right?"

"Daniel, would we get to your point any quicker if we took the bus?"

"Oh, very funny. What I'm getting at is... I just thought..." He took a deep breath. "Maybe it's time you had a go at writing something in the book yourself."

For the longest moment, the only sound was the ticking of the many clocks on the walls.

"Are you serious?" Susan asked in a whisper.

"Yeah. It's obvious you have a connection to the place, that you have talent. What's the point in any of this if I keep the fun all to myself?"

She threw herself forward again, hugging him tight.

"Alright, alright. You're going to break my ribs."

"Sorry."

He went to the desk, fixing his hair, and brought the *Book of Wonders* out from its drawer. When he placed the book on the desk, Susan stared down at the golden letters on the cover, and a strange, tingling pressure built up in her fingertips, like something was bursting to get out.

Daniel pulled his chair out, indicated that she should sit. She did. On her many visits, she'd never sat on this side of the desk. It felt strangely comfortable.

It felt right.

Daniel handed her a pen. "Go on then."

Susan took the pen and stared at it as if it were some strange foreign object. She had not been expecting this. Since her very first visit to the Emporium, she had longed to write in the *Book of Wonders*. As she opened the old book, flipped through its many pages, she recognised here and there the Wonders she had visited. She questioned if this was a dream. It seemed too wonderful to be true.

When she reached an empty page at last, she found that her mind was similarly blank. She laughed and shook her head. "I don't believe it. I can't think of anything!"

"You will," said Daniel. "We have plenty of time."

Susan stared and stared at the page, waiting for something to come into her head. And then, just as she was about to give up, it happened. She wrote quickly, almost frightened that the idea might desert her before she finished, the scratch of the fountain-pen nib on the textured paper making a delicious sound as she worked.

"There," she said at last. "Done. Do you want to read it? Make sure it's OK?"

"No," said Daniel with a smile. "I want a surprise. Besides, I know it'll be better than OK."

They walked for almost half an hour through the Carnival of Wonders, wandering the tangled pathways between the high canvas tents, only stopping so that Susan could sample Anything Soda. A cheerful vendor ladled the smoking liquid into a goblet from a huge cauldron.

"Whatever flavour you think of, the Anything Soda will become," Daniel told her.

Hesitant, Susan slowly raised the goblet to her mouth and closed her eyes. "It is my birthday, so how about birthday cake?" She touched the goblet to her lips, took a sip. The soda was cold as ice, and the saccharine taste of birthday cake, of sponge and buttercream, flooded her mouth, made her every taste bud tingle. "It's amazing!"

"Of course it is." Daniel laughed and he took her arm. "Come on, I'm dying to see this new Wonder of yours."

The tent was square and neat, made of black canvas with a tall pointed roof. A heavy gold curtain hung at the entrance. When they pushed through, they found themselves standing on the bank of a gentle river, open countryside spreading out before them. It was night, but the moon was so huge and bright in the sky that they could see quite clearly by its light, which scattered over the lapping surface of the water.

"It's exactly as I wrote it," said Susan, her voice almost a whisper.

"Did you think it wouldn't be?"

"I don't know. I've seen you write new Wonders in the book lots of times, but… I suppose I just thought it might not work so well for me." She crouched, let her fingers run through the wild grass, and was struck by how real it felt, how substantial. These were her thoughts, this place entirely dreamed up in her imagination, and yet here she stood. The magic of it, the sheer rush of excitement and awe and pride, swelled in her chest until she thought she might burst.

"So?" said Daniel. "What is it? What actually happens in here?"

Susan straightened up, glanced around at the sky, and smiled. "Well, if it goes like it's supposed to…" She held out a hand, palm up, and felt the first drops of rain hit her skin. Slowly, the rain became heavier, the droplets growing, the gentle patter becoming a drum. And as the rain fell upon them, rather than run for the cover of an oak tree as they might normally do, they stood on the riverbank and let the rain hit them and looked at their hands and clothes in astonishment.

"We're dry..." said Daniel.

The rain was now a torrent, but Daniel and Susan's clothes and face and hair remained as dry as if it was a summer day.

Not only that, but as the raindrops hit them, their hearts felt lighter and lighter, and their spirits soared, until they each felt incredibly happy, almost as if a beam of sunshine would burst from them.

Susan looked at Daniel, and he looked back at her, his eyes twinkling. "It's happiness, isn't it?" he said. "It's raining happiness!"

Susan nodded and smiled, and then she was laughing, holding her open hand out to catch the droplets of happiness falling from the sky. "This has been a day I'll remember forever," she told him. "I've been so happy, so lucky. And when I was thinking about what to write in the book, I realised suddenly that not everybody gets to have days like today. Not everyone gets to be as happy as I am. I know that every so often people will come to the Nowhere Emporium who need to feel that happiness more than anything, for all sorts of reasons. And so, this is where they'll come. This is where they'll smile and feel light, even if only for a little while. And maybe some of the happiness will stay with them when they leave..." She stopped because the look on Daniel's face was difficult to read. "That is... if it's alright with you."

He blinked, and stared at her, and she realised that there were tears in his eyes. "Alright? Susan... this is more than alright. It's extraordinary. Feeling like this…" He held his own hand out now, a little smaller than hers, and let the drops of happiness patter into his waiting palm. "Feeling as happy as I do now… truly happy… I can't remember the last time."

As Susan watched him, the thought struck her for the very first time that Daniel was really still just a boy, and that as wondrous as the Emporium was, he was all alone. He had his staff, of course, but that wasn't the same as having a family.

"What?" he said, noticing that she was watching him. "What is it?"

"Oh. Nothing. I just…"

She did not finish, because a rumble filled the air, so deep and powerful that it drowned out even the thrum of the rain and shook the ground. Daniel grabbed Susan by the hand and rushed her back through the door to the Carnival of Wonders.

"What was that?" she asked.

He brought the book out of his coat, began flipping through the pages, his brow furrowing with concern and concentration. "I don't know. I think…" He looked up at her as if something had just occurred to him. "Stay here. I'll be back."

"But, Daniel, what is it? What's…"

And just like that, he turned and dashed away, disappearing into the maze of colourful tents, leaving her alone.

CHAPTER 14

A GHOST

Glasgow, 1996, the Same Night

There was one tent in the entire Emporium that customers could never find. One place that was off limits to outsiders.

The Fountain.

Once, Daniel had hidden it in a small patch of woodland within the Carnival. But the Fountain had been breached then, and so he had moved it here. Unlike the majority of tents in this magical place, this one was small and plain, its red canvas unremarkable in every way. No stripes of purple or gold. No high roof. No glittering signpost proclaiming the Wonder beyond the entrance. Just a little red tent.

When he entered, Daniel found himself standing on the familiar surface of a frozen pond, his feet crunching on snow and ice. The cold nipped at his nose, and the scent was that of a crisp winter morning. The air was still, and the gentle sound of birdsong echoed all about.

In the centre of the frozen pond stood three tiers of circular stone within an ornate circular low wall.

Flowing over those stone circles was a thin liquid so silvery and bright that it seemed almost to glow. This was the fuel that powered the Emporium, the pure imagination that came from Daniel's mind and became magic as it passed over the stones.

As he approached, Daniel stared at the fountain, his mouth a little open. He had never seen it like this. Normally, the imagination flowing over the stones was a gentle babble. Now, it had become a rush, foaming and bubbling, even overflowing, pouring over the low circular wall and running onto the ice.

"So much magic."

"Oh," said Daniel with a start. "Hello, Caleb. I didn't hear you come in."

Caleb, the fire-breather, stood at Daniel's side, huge and bearlike, staring into the fountain. "What do you think is causing this sudden rush of power?"

Daniel was holding the book, his fingers tracing the golden letters on the cover. "You feel it?"

Caleb nodded. "Of course. I'm part of the Emporium. That's why I came. I wanted to see what was going on."

"It's Susie," Daniel said.

Caleb frowned. "The girl who has been visiting? What about her?"

"Yeah. You know I've been looking for someone to share the Emporium with for ages – ever since Ellie left. You and Ted practically begged me to, remember? Well, I think Susie might be the person."

"Really?" Caleb's face lit up. "That's wonderful!"

"Yeah. Except…"

"Except what?"

"She's powerful."

"Powerful?"

"Yeah. Her ability is off the scale. She's already better than me – and that's without anyone actually teaching her."

"And that frightens you?"

"What? No! I don't think so. Maybe. Just a wee bit."

"And she's responsible for all this imagination?" Caleb indicated the overflowing liquid in the fountain.

"Yeah. First time she's written in the book. And there's something else."

"There is?"

"Yeah. Earlier, after she'd finished writing her first Wonder, it felt like the book wanted to stay with her. Like it… preferred her or something."

When these words spilled from his mouth, Daniel realised how it must sound: that he was jealous; that he did not want to share *his* Emporium with anyone. And he was ashamed to admit that, although he *had* been searching for someone to share the Emporium with, he was a little upset that the person he'd found was making it all look so easy.

Caleb gave him a sad smile. "Daniel, it's alright to be protective of the Emporium, but you must not shut yourself away from the world from fear of losing it. Such a strategy did not end well for Lucien Silver, if you remember?"

"Of course," Daniel replied.

"You know how it works," said Caleb. "The Nowhere Emporium is yours, and it will remain yours until you decide that you have had enough. So what if this girl is a natural at magic? So what if she becomes more powerful than you? Celebrate that. Learn from her as she will learn from you. Make the Emporium even better, even stronger."

Daniel smiled up at the bare-chested fire-breather. "Thanks, Caleb. I can always rely on you, can't I?"

Caleb turned his gaze back to the silvery liquid, took a deep breath of the crisp air. "Until the end, Daniel Holmes. Until the very end."

Daniel had instructed Susie to stay put.

Naturally, she had not paid the least bit of attention and was now wandering among the tents in the Carnival of Wonders.

If he's going to run off and leave me, she thought, *then I'm going to have a bit of fun.* But which Wonder to visit?

Which one…

Which one…

That one.

The tent was not tall, or colourful. Nothing about it attracted attention. But that was what made it stand out. It was made of plain, worn white canvas that rippled in the warm evening breeze. The signpost outside the tent was scratched so much that the name of the Wonder inside was illegible. As Susie stood outside the tent and stared at the entrance, a strange electricity passed through her; she felt compelled to get closer, and as she did, a breath of perfumed air came from the entranceway and stroked her face.

She was close enough to the entrance curtain that the tip of her nose brushed the material. She took a glance over her shoulder. Still no Daniel. That made her mind up. She walked forward and pushed into the tent.

She was standing in an empty room. There were no windows. The floorboards were worn and creaked beneath her feet. The floral wallpaper, which looked like it had once been rich and vibrant, was faded and peeling. All was lit by the dim glow of gas lamps in rusted sconces on the walls. The only other feature in the room, besides the exit, was a door in the far wall.

Susie walked towards the door, reached for the handle and found that it was locked.

She made a fist and knocked three times.

Silence.

Then, from the other side of the door, someone knocked back.

Bump.

Bump.

Bump.

Susie took a step back. Her mouth was dry. "Hello?"

A pause. Then a man's voice, low and smooth. "Hello."

"Who's there?"

"I might ask the same," said the voice.

"Susie. My name is Susie. What are you doing behind that door?"

"What, Susie, are *you* doing behind *that* door?"

"I'm exploring."

"Ah."

"Why is this door locked?"

"Why do you think?"

"I don't know."

"Well," said the voice, "why does one usually lock a door?"

"Um… to keep people out?"

"Perhaps," said the voice. "Or…"

Susie took a sharp breath. "To keep you in?"

"And there we have it."

Susie stroked her chin – an involuntary movement. She took a small faltering step towards the door, and another, and another, until she was close enough that she imagined she could hear the man's breath on the other side. Or maybe she wasn't imagining. "Are you saying you're a prisoner?"

No answer.

"But why would Daniel keep you prisoner? I don't believe that at all."

"Tell me, Susie, do you always make up your mind before you know all the facts?"

"What? No."

"And do you know Daniel well enough to make such an assumption?"

Susie began to argue, but she could not find the words. The more she thought about it, the more she realised that she really did not know Daniel very well at all. Still, she could not conceive that he'd do something like this. "If you're telling the truth, why has he trapped you?"

"Because he is frightened of me."

"And why is that? What did you do to him?"

She could hear the smile in his voice when he next spoke. "The only thing I ever did to Daniel Holmes was show him that I'm a better magician. He saw me as a threat. He was jealous. He, quite wrongly I might add, became paranoid and began to believe that I wanted the Emporium for myself. And so he locked me away." A long moment of silence, and then the man added, "You would be wise to avoid the same fate, Susie."

"Me?" Susie shook her head as if there was a fly buzzing about her hair. "What in the world would Daniel ever want to lock me away for?"

She heard a soft scratching sound on the other side of the door, and in her mind's eye saw a hand pressed against the wood, wishing that it could feel the warmth of another's touch. She felt pity.

"I do not think, Susie, that you have the faintest clue quite how powerful you are – or how that power will eventually drive our dear Mr Holmes mad. Be careful. Promise me?"

"But I…"

"Promise me, please."

"OK. I promise."

"Good. Now, go on. Get out of here. He's coming. Whatever you do, don't let him know you found me. If he finds out, who knows what he might do."

Her head all a-spin, Susie hurried out of the tent, back to the still warmth of the carnival's forever twilight. As she walked away, she looked back and saw that the little tent was gone.

"There you are! I've been looking for ages!" Susie jumped at the sight of Daniel hurrying around a corner. "You OK?" he asked. "You look like you've just seen the devil."

"I'm fine," she said, feeling anything but.

Daniel rubbed his hands together. "Good. So where do you want to go next?"

Susie suddenly wanted to be at home in her warm, safe bedroom, knowing Mum was in the next room and Dad downstairs watching TV. "Actually, Daniel, I feel a bit iffy. I guess I must've had too much birthday cake or something. You mind if I go home?"

"Oh. OK. Of course," he said, and she could tell he was trying his best to hide his disappointment. "Whatever you want. Let's get you back."

It was a strange feeling walking beside him now. She had never, ever thought of him as anything but a friend, a gentle soul. But one encounter with the man behind the door had made her think deeply about Daniel Holmes and the Nowhere Emporium. Questions that she had never asked bubbled to the surface: What did Daniel really want? Why did he keep coming back? Was it possible that he'd eventually get jealous of her and lock her away too? She tried to shake these thoughts away, but they stuck in her head like splinters.

When they reached the shopfront at last, Daniel opened the door to the cold night.

"I guess I'll see you soon?" he said.

"Yeah. Of course."

"Hey, Susie?"

"Yeah?"

"You sure nothing's wrong? Nothing happened to you while I was gone, did it?"

She gave him what she hoped was a cheerful punch on the arm. "Don't be daft! I'll see you next time." She turned and began walking away, back towards the warm comfort of home, relief and sadness filling her up. Then, when she reached the front door, she turned back, and saw that Daniel was still watching. Normally she would have thought this sweet. Tonight, she wondered if he was watching because he suspected something.

Forcing a smile, she gave him a wave and snuck back inside, glad to be home.

CHAPTER 15

A DOOR IN THE SKY

The Nowhere Emporium, Present Day

Mirren, Luke and Robyn were falling. No time to think or react. No time to be frightened. No time for anything.

Deafening sound. The roaring, whistling shriek of cutting through the air.

The shock of feeling the harshness of the air itself, like it was a solid thing, ripping at their skin, pushing their lips back over their teeth.

Mirren's hand was still, somehow, clutching Luke's. The warmth of it seemed, as they tumbled through the clear blue sky, like the only real thing left in the world. Far, far below, the ground was racing towards them.

The ground... and something else.

Their hands were wrenched apart when they landed. Not on the hard earth, but on a surface as soft and yielding as a mountain of cotton wool. The fluffy white material enveloped Mirren in a warm blanket as she sunk into it, and then, gently, bounced her back up.

"Luke?"

"Here!"

He was a few metres away, trying to clamber out of the deep indent he had made in the soft surface. Mirren bounded over to help him; it proved difficult to manoeuvre about on this stuff, a strange mixture of snow and springy cotton wool. She gave him her hand, helped him out.

"Help! Help!"

"Robyn? Robyn, where are you?"

"Over... here! Quick!"

When they found her, it was difficult not to laugh. Her head and upper body were buried in the white fluff, her backside sticking out, legs kicking, horrible sparkling slippers shining in the light of the sun.

"You grab one leg," said Mirren through a stifled chuckle. "I'll get the other."

Luke nodded, and Mirren loved him for not offering to pull Robyn out by himself. He was the only person, apart from Mum, who realised that she could do things as well as everyone else, that she wasn't some sort of ornament that had to be wrapped up and protected.

Mirren grabbed one of Robyn's ankles, Luke the other, and they pulled and pulled until, finally, Robyn came loose and together they tumbled backwards, bouncing and rolling until they all managed to scramble up.

Robyn's face was almost glowing with embarrassment. She looked from Mirren to Luke, her watery blue eyes wide. "Don't tell anyone about that. I'm warning you!"

"What?" said Mirren.

"Don't dare mention what just happened to anyone. If you do, I'll… I'll…"

"First of all," said Mirren, her hand on her hip, "you're welcome. Secondly, not everyone's brain works like yours. Believe it or not, embarrassing you is the last thing on my mind right now. And thirdly, Robyn, do you think anyone would believe us even if we did tell them that you got stuck in a cloud and your backside was waving about in the air?"

Robyn's eyes flashed with anger, and then her expression softened. "Sorry. I should have said thanks. And my mind doesn't always work like that. I just thought, after how mean I've been to you two, you might want to get your own back." She stopped, held up a finger. "Wait. Go back a second or two. Did you just say we're on a *cloud?*"

"We're on a white fluffy thing floating in the sky," said Mirren, pointing up over Robyn's shoulder towards a huge whipped candyfloss spire. "What else can it be?"

"But clouds aren't like this," reasoned Robyn. "They're just water vapour, aren't they?" She pressed her foot into the surface, leaving a deep indent that slowly sprung back. "This is impossible."

Luke nodded. "Under normal circumstances, I'd agree with you—" He stopped, frowned and shook his head. "I can't believe I just admitted that."

Mirren's eyes flicked all about. "I don't think the word 'impossible' exists in this place."

Robyn raised a hand. "Um. Question."

"Just one?" said Luke.

"Well, actually, about a million – but one really, really important one. And that is… how do we get down from here?"

Mirren looked at her best friend, who could only shrug. "She's right, Mir. We're stuck. What are we going to do?"

"Why you asking *me*?" Mirren suddenly realised that there was a sort of expectancy in the way both Luke and Robyn were looking at her – like they were waiting for her to make a decision. As if she was somehow in charge. She looked around. "Well, I guess the compass brought us here for a reason, right? Let's explore a bit and see if we can find anything."

"Should we split up?" asked Luke.

Robyn tutted in exasperation. "Oh, yeah, great idea. Let's copy the stupid heroes of every bad movie we've ever watched and split up, then get picked off one by one."

"You don't have to be sarcastic," said Luke. "Hey, Mir, wait up!"

It was a strange feeling, half walking, half bouncing over a candyfloss island in the sky. They covered the perimeter first, taking care not to go too near the edge, which fell away for thousands of metres to the ground. Looking over it made Mirren quite dizzy. After that they moved inwards, around the base of the great fluffy spire.

"What do you think happened to Ted?" Robyn stared up the cliff face. "Do you think he's…?"

"I think we should keep looking before those Nightmares figure out a way of getting down here," said Mirren.

"But what are we even looking for?"

"I don't know! Maybe a door, or…" Mirren stopped. The beginning of an idea was forming in her mind. "Robyn, what did Ted say about that key he gave you?"

Robyn brought the little key out of the pocket of her oversized dressing gown, and they stared at it as it nestled in her hand.

"Something about doors, wasn't it?" said Luke.

"That's right." Robyn's eyes narrowed in concentration.

"He said, 'This key opens doors where there are none'. How d'you think that works, then?"

"Back when we were running from the treasure monster," said Mirren, "Ted helped us get away through a door from nowhere. He must have used this key."

Robyn held the key by its book-shaped handle. "I wonder…" She moved it forward, as if she was slipping it into a keyhole. The key began to glow, and Robyn's face was such a picture of stunned amazement that Mirren almost laughed out loud.

But even though the key was glowing, there was no sign of any door.

"What should I do?"

Mirren's brain was clicking through the gears again. "Try turning it, Robyn – like you're unlocking a lock."

Robyn nodded. She turned the key. A deep, satisfying *click* rang out, and after that a dazzling rectangular outline appeared in the air. There was a fizzing sound, a bright flash, and there it was – a door in the sky, glossy and red, with a gold doorknob.

Robyn stared at the key in her trembling hand. It was no longer glowing. "I can't believe that worked. Where do you think it goes?"

Mirren stepped forward, butterflies fluttering in her belly. She reached for the handle; it was warm against her skin. "Only one way to find out."

CHAPTER 16

THE SNAKE CHARMER

The Nowhere Emporium, Present Day

They stepped onto plush red carpet, almost as soft as the surface of the magical cloud they'd just left. The door slammed behind them and was gone, leaving them standing huddled together in a grand corridor, all red and gold and marble, lined on either side with jewel-encrusted doors and paintings in the sort of ornate frames Mirren had only ever seen in the art gallery in Glasgow.

"Oh no," said Luke. "We're back in that maniac's palace, aren't we?"

"You don't think that treasure thingy will come after us again, do you?" Robyn grabbed his arm, and

Mirren felt a surprising jolt of jealousy run through her, but it was gone in a moment when the dial of the compass swung around and glowed brightly.

"I guess we go this way," said Luke.

It seemed that the corridor would never end. They walked and walked, and still the compass pointed them onward. All the while, solemn faces stared down at them from the paintings. Something about them gave Mirren a bad feeling. And then it hit her.

"They're all the same guy!"

Robyn gave her a sideways look. "What? What are you on about?"

"The portraits. Look!" Mirren went to the nearest painting, depicting a tall, broad man reading a book. Then she hurried up the passageway to the next portrait, which featured the same man eating at a grand table. "See? And this one…" She ran on, indicating a painting of the same fellow on horseback. "And this, and this, and this…"

Every portrait was of one man. He had neatly cropped silver hair and a square, determined jaw. His eyes were an eerie ice-blue, almost aglow.

"Do you think it's Vindictus Sharpe?" Luke approached one of the paintings, reached out.

"Don't touch it!" The words escaped Mirren before she could think, and she was shocked by how she had screamed them.

"Jeezo, Mirren," said Robyn. "You didn't need to shout at him like that. They're just paintings… aren't they?"

Mirren didn't answer at first, because another of the portraits had caught her attention. She began to move towards it, unease rising in her throat. "I'm sorry. I just have a bad feeling about these paintings. If it is Sharpe, I don't think we should be messing with them." She had come quite near to the portrait; it was a close-up of the man's head and shoulders, but he was not looking out of the frame. His head was tilted downwards, and his gaze rested somewhere on the floor below, out of the picture.

Mirren took another step, and another, not knowing quite why it was pulling her in, or what she was looking for, and each step made her blood run colder in her veins.

The man's head snapped up.

His icy blue eyes met Mirren's, and she screamed and staggered back as a hand appeared on the canvas and began to push out from inside the painting.

"Run!"

Sharpe's deep, growling laugh echoed after them as they spun away and ran.

"Mir! Look!"

Luke was pointing back down the passageway. Nightmares were spilling out of Sharpe's portrait, inky masses of arms and legs and teeth tearing after them, hissing and spitting and moaning.

"We're dead!" wailed Robyn. "Oh, we're going to die in this awful shop!"

"The key, Robyn. Where's the key?"

She pulled the key out of her dressing gown. "I think we'll have to stop to use it."

Panting, they skidded to a stop on the thick red carpet.

"Hurry!" said Luke, casting a glance back down the passage towards the onrushing Nightmares.

Robyn took the key and moved it forwards in the air, slipping it into an imaginary lock. She turned the key, and the loud *click* sounded out. Then there was the glowing frame, and a flash, and a door appeared. Robyn yanked it open. "Go!"

The door slammed shut behind them and vanished. Mirren and her friends collapsed onto the ground: a hard, arid patch of bleached grass. They lay sprawled out, taking great breaths of warm air, until they felt ready to stand again. When at last they looked around properly, they found that they were standing in the remains of what might once have been a grand carnival or circus. Faded, half-collapsed tents surrounded them. The air was silent and warm and still, the twilight sky vast and twinkling. A faint whisper of popcorn drifted on the air, an echo of another time perhaps.

"Good work, Robyn," said Luke. Robyn's face flushed. Luke held the compass out again, watched the glowing dial settle. "We should probably keep moving, yeah? Wonder what this place is – looks like where circuses go to die." He made to set off, and then stopped. "What's the matter, Mir?"

Mirren had hung back, hoping nobody would notice the tears in her eyes. Her throat was tight, her head swimming with panic. "I'm just having a wee moment, that's all." But now their attention was on her, she was struggling to hold back the emotion she'd so far kept in check. "I mean… how are we ever supposed to find my mum? Look at the size of this place. Look at who's trying to stop us, what we're up against. We're only three kids, Lukasz! Do we really have a chance? What if I never see her again? What if she's… gone?"

Luke walked over and stood right in front of her, frowning. "Mirren, since the day we met in Primary One, I've never seen you give up on anything."

"I know, but…"

"But?" said Luke. "No. No buts. When you were in a car crash as a baby, and the doctors thought you wouldn't make it, did you give up then?"

"Well, no… but—"

"I said no buts! That crash took away your arm, and your dad, but have you ever let that stop you from doing anything? Have you?"

"No."

"Exactly! You made the basketball team. You learned to swim. You helped me build a treehouse in the woods. You're better at video games than I could ever be – even if I had three arms."

Mirren laughed at this and dabbed her eyes with a knuckle.

"You're going to find your mum, Mir," he went on. "I know it. And we'll be here to help every step of the way, right, Robyn?"

Robyn nodded, and seemed to look at Mirren like she was seeing her in a new light.

"Now, come on," said Luke. "Let's keep going."

He turned and walked, but Robyn held back, waiting for Mirren, much to Mirren's surprise.

"I didn't know… about the accident. I mean, I knew a little bit. I knew there had been some sort of accident, and that's how you lost your arm when you were wee. But I didn't realise that's how your dad… I'm sorry."

Mirren smiled. She felt lighter after Luke's talk. She could always rely on him to cheer her up. "Thanks. But there's nothing to be sorry for, Robyn. And Luke's right – we'll find my mum. I'm glad you guys are here to help me."

"Even me?" asked Robyn.

Mirren chuckled. "Yeah. Believe it or not, Robyn, even you."

They followed the compass through a maze of ruined tents, passing the abandoned remains of stalls and broken signposts, until the sound of a popping fire echoed in the still air. Mirren and her companions crept into the skeletal remains of a once-proud big top to find a small campsite. From their hiding place among the fallen poles and hanging strips of ragged canvas they spied a woman sitting at the campfire, her back turned to them.

"Should we speak to her?" whispered Robyn.

"I don't know," said Luke. "The compass is telling us to keep walking, but what if she's with Sharpe?"

But Mirren shook her head. "I don't think she is. She's not one of those Nightmares, is she? It seems to me like she's hiding here. And look. On her hand!"

The woman lifted a metal cup to her mouth, and by the flickering light of the campfire it was easy to see a tattoo on the dark brown skin of her hand. The very same symbol Ted had marked on his own metal skin.

"The League of the Book," said Robyn.

"Whoever is there, come out. Now." The woman's voice was calm and clear; she did not look up from the fire, did not even bother to move at all. "You have ten seconds."

Mirren, Luke and Robyn shared frightened looks. Of course, it occurred to them to run, but this woman looked lean and athletic, and they didn't fancy their chances of outrunning her through a maze of tents that she probably knew very well.

They slunk out of the shadows, approaching the campfire.

"Come around so I can see you," said the woman.

They circled around, so that they stood on the opposite side of the fire to her. She was stern-faced and beautiful, with shortly cropped black hair and deep brown eyes. Her clothes were ragged and patched. They stood before her as she looked them up and down, her face expressionless. "Who are you?"

"Please don't hurt us," Robyn blurted out.

"I am not going to hurt you," said the woman. She made a strange movement with her hand then, a slight wave of the fingers. From the surrounding shadows there came a soft, slithering sound.

Luke let out a yelp.

Snakes, dozens of them, were coming from the dark. There were all shapes and sizes: grass snakes, pythons, adders – even a cobra. They moved slowly, surrounding the campfire, tasting the air.

"I hate snakes." Luke was sweating, trembling.

Mirren took one of his hands and Robyn took the other. "You said you wouldn't hurt us."

The woman stood up. She was tall, over six feet, with a graceful neck and limbs. She raised a perfect eyebrow. "I won't hurt you. But I can't say the same for the snakes, should they decide you are lying to me.

I'll ask again. Who are you?"

Mirren found her voice. "I'm just a normal kid from the outside world. We all are. But Daniel Holmes brought us here tonight. My mum's in the Emporium somewhere too, you see, and Daniel Holmes told me she's in trouble, that we have to help him—"

"You spoke to Daniel Holmes?" said the woman. "Tonight?"

"He sent a message out to us," said Mirren. "Look. He gave us these. Show her, guys."

They each produced the feather Daniel Holmes had sent to guide them to the Nowhere Emporium. The woman gazed at the feathers. After a long moment, she made that strange hand gesture again, and the snakes slipped back into the surrounding shadows. "I'm sorry about that," she said. "But after everything that's gone on, I can't be too careful."

"Um, who are you?" asked Luke.

"Come. Sit. It's OK, I promise."

They sat by the fire; the warmth of it was comforting.

"My name is Anja," said the woman.

"I'm Mirren. This is Lukasz, and this is Robyn."

"And you say you've come to help Daniel?"

"Yeah. And to rescue my mum, Susan Feather. But, you see, we don't know how we're going to do that. I mean, we have this compass, and Ted gave Robyn a key…"

"You saw Ted?" Anja's eyes grew wide. "He's OK?"

"We don't know. We had to leave in a hurry. Sharpe's Nightmares came after us and Ted... he was really brave. He made sure we got away."

Anja closed her eyes for a moment. "I see. And you say he gave you a key?"

"This one," said Robyn, reaching into her dressing gown. "It opens doors where we need... Oh. That's weird. It's all rusted." She opened her palm. The key, only hours ago shining and solid, had become gnarled and rusted. It looked like it might crumble at any moment.

"It's Sharpe's doing," said Anja. "He poisons everything in this place. It looks like you might only be able to use that key once more. Twice if you're lucky."

"What about our feathers?" asked Mirren. "And Luke's compass?"

"You say Daniel gave those to you this very night?"

"Yeah. He said he put the last of his power into them."

Anja let out a long, sad sigh. "They are new objects. Sharpe has not poisoned them yet. But if they stay in the Emporium long enough, they will rot away too."

"But what does Sharpe actually want?" said Mirren. She could feel herself becoming angry again. "Why has he taken my mum? Ted said she'd been here before, that she had... had some connection to the shop?"

147

Anja sat back, her hands on her knees. "Susie Anderson visited the Emporium several times over the years. There is no doubting that she shared a powerful bond with the place. In fact, I believe Daniel was considering making her his apprentice."

"Mum?" said Mirren in disbelief. "Working here?"

"Indeed," said Anja. "Obviously that did not work out. But perhaps Sharpe lured her back to the place so he can use her power. There's no doubt his grip on the Emporium has tightened since she arrived. The League of the Book is now almost gone. Only pockets of resistance linger on, and little islands of safety like this, where I've been trapped for so long."

"So Sharpe doesn't know about this place?" said Luke.

Anja took a breath and indicated the surrounding big top. "The Emporium changes with every owner. The shop always takes the form that best reflects its master. With Mr Silver, it was all black brick and shadow and lamplight. He had a taste for the dramatic, but it was a little depressing for my liking. When Daniel took over, he transformed the place into a huge carnival. The Carnival of Wonders. That was more like it! A never-ending maze of tents, each containing a Wonder beyond description."

"That's what this is?" asked Robyn. "A bit left over from Daniel's Emporium?"

"Quite so. A bubble of safety – though for how much longer I don't know. It's becoming more unstable by the minute. Sharpe's version of the Emporium tells you all you need to know about the man, or what is left of him. A grand palace filled with riches. Infinite corridors of lavish gold, every painting one of Sharpe himself."

Mirren stared into the fire. "I can't believe Mum knew about this place and never told me."

Anja shrugged. "Everyone has secrets, Mirren Feather."

"Will you help us find her, Anja? Please?"

A pause. Anja was about to say something, but the dial of the compass spun around once and glowed brighter than ever, catching her attention. She stood up, sniffed at the air and wheeled around to face the children again. "Something has changed in the carnival; I can feel it. Sharpe's Nightmares are here."

CHAPTER 17
SNOW GLOBES

The Nowhere Emporium, Present Day

"I thought you said this was a safe place?" Robyn pressed her hand to her chest and looked warily all about. "Why does everything here want to kill us?"

"It *was* a safe place," Anja said, with a mixture of shock and indignation. "Come. Out of the tent." Then, to Luke, she said, "What does the compass say?"

"That way." He pointed.

"Well then, come on."

They crept out of the big top, back into the warm evening, and followed the dial of the compass through the twisting graveyard of leaning, ragged tents, now and then hearing the distant sound of swarming Nightmares.

"Around this corner," said Luke. "There! It's pointing to that purple tent!" He set out to run, but Anja grabbed him, dragged him back by the collar, and rushed the children into a hiding spot behind a long-abandoned popcorn stand. She held a finger to her lips to quiet them. An icy blast of fear hit Mirren when she heard a mix of familiar sounds. They began with ragged, wet breathing and then, as it came nearer, graduated to growling and slurping and sniffing. A Nightmare.

Mirren felt her body go rigid. Luke's eyes were shut tight, and Robyn's hands seemed to be clasped in prayer.

The Nightmare came closer, closer, closer still; they heard its feet on the hard, patchy grass, smelled its rotten stench. If it discovered them, it would attack, and the noise would attract the others, maybe dozens of them, hundreds.

Mirren held her breath. She looked at Anja, who was crouched beside her. Anja's eyes stared back, and there was a great fierceness in them. She made that waving movement with her fingers.

The snake came from nowhere. Huge, as thick as a tree trunk, it passed inches from Mirren, a forked tongue shooting in and out from a head the size of a frying pan.

The sounds from the Nightmare, the sniffing and gargling, suddenly stopped. A grunt, a thump, and Anja stood up and signalled the children to do the same. When they came out from behind the cart, they saw the snake's massive body wrapped around the dark shape of the Nightmare, squeezing, until nothing remained but a dark stain on the grass.

Satisfied, Anja nodded to Luke, and then pointed to the entrance of the purple tent. "Lead the way."

The room beyond was dim and still and silent. At first, because their eyes were adjusting from the burning twilight sky, it seemed to Mirren and her friends that they had walked into empty blackness. But then shapes began to appear in their vision, glimmers of crystal light.

"There's something in the middle." Mirren took a few steps, and gas lamps blinked on all around the circumference of what was, in fact, a circular room. The lamps caught light one at a time, around and around, spiralling up and up, seemingly forever. In the centre of the room stood a huge column of stone, honeycombed with roughly cut compartments, and in these compartments sat the objects that they had seen glimmering in the dark.

"Snow globes." Mirren had reached the column, found the foot of a staircase that wrapped up and around the stone. She climbed slowly, her eyes feasting on the crystal globes sitting snugly in their compartments. There were so many, every single one as unique and enchanting as the last. No two were the same, either in size or design; the largest was the size of a beachball, the smallest no bigger than a marble.

"Do you think we can touch them?" she asked. Her fingers twitched.

"Careful, Mir," warned Luke. "It might be a trick. What if… I don't know, what if you get sucked in and trapped?"

"Or what if touching a snow globe brings out what's inside?" said Robyn.

"No," said Anja. "There is, I think, nothing to be fearful of in this Wonder. I have heard of it, you see – although this is my first visit."

Mirren had been staring into one of the globes. It was the size of an orange, and inside, two children sat under an apple tree reading a book on a perfect summer's day. "So, where are we?"

Until this moment, it had seemed that Anja was unflappable, that she was so used to the unpredictable danger of the Emporium, the magic and wonder, that nothing could surprise her. But this room had a strange effect on even her. Seemingly awestruck,

Anja wandered around, staring not just at the snow globes, but at the room itself, her gaze carrying far off up into the darkness.

"If I am right," she said, "and I have been around long enough to believe that I am, we are standing in the very first room Daniel Holmes created in the Nowhere Emporium." She joined Mirren on the winding staircase. As she climbed, her fingertips kissed many of the crystal spheres. She stopped beside Mirren, reached out a long, elegant arm and, with great care, brought out the globe Mirren had been looking at, the one containing the children reading under the apple tree. "I believe," she went on, "that every globe you see in this place contains a secret."

She held up the globe, and Mirren's eyes followed it, drank in every detail. As she gazed at the scene inside the delicate crystal casing, she could almost feel the warmth of the buttery sunshine, smell the summer grass, taste the sweet crunch of the apples. "How can there be secrets in all of these?"

"As I told you," said Anja, "everyone has secrets." Her voice was dripping with fascination. "Some people have secrets that they wish to forget, wish to seal away so that nobody can ever find out. This is a place to leave those secrets, a room to keep them safe until the end of time."

Robyn and Luke joined them on the spiral stairs.

"There are so many," Robyn said. She reached out and lifted a snow globe about the size of a snooker ball from its place in the honeycombed stone. "I wonder what this one is." Inside was a tiny battered suitcase. "Look, there's a name…" She held out the globe so that the others could see; on the wooden base of the snow globe was a small golden nameplate, engraved with the name 'Stanley Marigold'. "I wonder what old Stanley is hiding in his suitcase," she said, peering inside. "I'll bet he's… OH!"

Robyn's foot slipped on the edge of a step and she fell sideways. She somehow managed to right herself with the banister, but in the process let go of the snow globe. Everyone froze as it fell, seemingly forever, through the darkness. Finally, it hit the steps. But it did not smash. Instead, it bounced like a rubber ball, landing safely back in Robyn's waiting hands. She stared at it with wide eyes.

"Ah," said Anja. "I've heard about this. Only the person who leaves the secret can open it. We couldn't smash any of these snow globes, even if we had a hammer."

Luke, who had been examining a beachball-sized globe containing a bunch of colourful balloons, broke away from the rest of them, walked further up the steps and around the column of stone. As he passed, Mirren noticed that he was reading the compass once more, and she followed, not saying a word, not wanting to break Luke's concentration or the connection he seemed to share with the instrument.

The stairs were uneven; with his gaze firmly fixed on the dial of the compass, Luke's balance faltered several times, but he carried on regardless, climbing further and further. Mirren chanced a glance over the edge of the thin black railing. The spiral of blinking gas lamps reached down a dizzying distance to the floor below.

When Luke finally stopped, he wore a puzzled look. He checked and rechecked the compass. Then his gaze scanned the honeycombed stone directly in front of him, and after a long moment he took in one sharp, short breath. He reached out, and with trembling fingers, brought down a grapefruit-sized snow globe.

"What's that? Luke? What's wrong?"

He was holding the globe as if it was about to explode, staring at it in disbelief.

"It's your mum," he said in a gravelly whisper.

At first Mirren's brain did not compute. "What?"

"Mir… this one has your mum's name on it."

With great care, he turned the snow globe around and held it out. Mirren stared at it, nestling in his cupped palms. It was quite beautiful. A miniature fountain stood in the centre of what seemed to be a frozen pond. All around stood tall, bare trees covered in frost. A strange silver liquid was flowing over the fountain, sparkling, almost glowing. And there, beside the fountain, stood two figures. They were silhouetted against the dazzling sun, so Mirren could not make out their features, whichever way she turned the globe in her hands. She could only tell that one was a man, and the other a woman.

Upon the wooden base into which the snow globe was set was a golden nameplate. And on the nameplate, a name that Mirren recognised as well as her own.

Mum's name.

◦ Susan Feather ◦

She stared at that name, and a foreign thought hatched in her mind: she considered the fact that Mum had once been young, that she'd had a past, before Mirren came along, and that, somehow, the Emporium had been a meaningful part of it.

And there was something else to think about. Mum had left a secret in this tent. Which meant that Mum had been in the Emporium before, just as Anja and Ted had said. When? And why?

As Anja had suspected, Mum had secrets.

"Mir?"

Luke was still holding the snow globe out towards her. For some reason, she felt that touching it would not be right. She still did not take it.

"Mir," said Luke in a gentle, cajoling voice. "The compass led me to this secret. I think it wants you to have it."

"You do?" She stared into Luke's dark eyes and saw the kindness that had lived there always, the fierce loyalty to her. And she knew he would never do anything to hurt her.

She reached out almost in slow motion, and only when she touched the cool crystal of the globe did she realise that she had been holding her breath, as if she'd been expecting the thing to shatter.

She took the globe, examined the beautiful scene inside, squinted at the mysterious figures. If this was Mum's secret, then it was possible – likely even – that the woman was her.

"What's that?" Robyn and Anja had finally caught up, and Robyn was peering at the globe in Mirren's hands.

"The compass led me to it," said Luke. "It belongs to Mirren's mum."

"I wonder if it's a clue about where she is?" said Robyn.

Mirren had been in her own bubble of contemplation, but Robyn's words popped it like a needle. "You could be right!" She held the globe out in her open palms. "Anja, do you recognise the place inside?"

"That is the Fountain," she said, her voice low, reverent. "It is, perhaps, the most important of all the

Wonders in the Nowhere Emporium. It is... how can I say it... the engine of the place. The Fountain is where imagination becomes pure magic."

Mirren stared into the crystal sphere, her heart fluttering. "That's the Fountain? Ted said something about that. He told us the League of the Book think that's where Sharpe is keeping Mum, but they can't find it. Sharpe has hidden it away. Have you heard the same?"

Anja took a moment to consider. "I've been trapped here for so long, unable to find a way back to the League, that I have lost all touch. But if Ted said it, I believe him."

Robyn gave a snort of exasperation. "How can you lose a room? How is that a thing?"

Anja held up a finger to quiet her. "Well, my snippy little friend, the fact is that the rules you know, the rules that apply to your world, do not apply here. In the Emporium – especially now, when it is so unstable – time and space and chemistry and physics, the laws of the universe, can be bent and broken, can be turned inside out and back again in the blink of an eye. It is, therefore, quite normal for tents or rooms to move, for Wonders to leak into one another, for entire floors to disappear, only to come back several miles away from their original location."

"That," said Robyn, "sounds like my mum's worst nightmare. She loses the plot if I move a pen! If entire rooms in my house started moving around, I reckon she'd explode. Like, properly explode with rage."

The situation was, of course, grave. But the way in which Robyn said this, combined with her wide-eyed, serious face, made Mirren chuckle.

"Think about it," Anja went on. "If you were Vindictus Sharpe, if all that was left of you, your soul, was connected to the Emporium forever, and you wanted to rule the place until the end of time, which room above all others would you cherish and protect?"

"The room that makes it all possible," said Mirren. "The engine of the place!"

"Exactly. But now you're here, with that compass and a secret linked to the Fountain, I am daring to hope again that we will find Sharpe and end his reign."

"It almost sounds like you want to fight him," said Robyn with a nervous laugh.

Anja looked at her, puzzled. "How else are we supposed to get the Emporium back?"

By the glowing dial of Luke's compass, they ascended the staircase further still, climbing for what seemed like hours. Their legs began to burn, and their lungs screamed for air. The higher they got, the colder it became, until every breath was painfully sharp. This high up, a thin coating of frost lay on everything, making the steps slippery, hiding the insides of the snow globes beneath twinkling ice crystals.

Nobody said a word. All concentration and willpower was now focussed solely on moving forward, carrying on.

A loud *clang* rang out far below, and Mirren and her friends froze in place. Anja put a finger to her lips, and then pointed to her ear. They strained to listen, trained their ears as best they could down into the far-off darkness.

Was that...

Faint, rushing footsteps. Lots of them. And a whispering, ragged hiss.

The Nightmares had found them.

The whites of Anja's eyes were clearly visible in the gloom, standing out against the thick black liner she wore. "You must use the key again," she told Robyn.

Robyn nodded, went first to the wrong pocket of her dressing gown and then the correct one, struggling to untangle the key from the lining.

"They're coming!" Luke peered over the bannister. Mirren did the same and at once wished she hadn't: a mass of black shapes was rushing up the staircase, screeching, knocking secrets from their place in the stone column, sending them crashing down.

"Hurry, Robyn!"

"I'm trying! There!" With a ripping sound, the key came free from her pocket, and she thrust it forward into an imaginary lock.

The first Nightmare came screaming around the staircase. Mirren acted purely on instinct; grabbing the bannister tightly, she lashed out a foot with all the strength she had. Her kick landed on the head of the Nightmare, sending the creature tumbling back, taking out the others just behind it.

Robyn had turned the key. The blazing outline of a door was appearing.

Anja waved a hand, and from the honeycombed stone column, among the many snow globes, came her snakes. Hundreds of them came lashing out of the holes in the stone, biting the Nightmares, coiling around them.

A flash, and the door was fully formed. Robyn threw it open, and they ran towards it, up the few steps to where it waited in the centre of the staircase. Robyn was through, and then Luke, holding Mirren's hand…

Something cold clamped around her ankle. She screamed as her hand slipped out of Luke's grip and his arm disappeared through the door. A Nightmare was pulling her back. Stranded on her belly, the weight of the Nightmare pressing down upon her, Mirren screamed and kicked and spat. She thought of Mum, of how she had to get to her. She struggled around, her arm raised to her face, shielding her from the Nightmare's grasping black fingers. Its featureless face opened up, and a long tongue lashed at the air.

Mirren kicked and kicked again; the Nightmare was heavy, but she wriggled free and landed another kick, and another. All around there were dark shapes, spitting mouths, snakes striking out, biting, squeezing, screeches of anger and hunger and pain...

A warm hand around her wrist, and suddenly Mirren was on her feet, looking into the faces of Robyn and Luke. Her friends had come back for her.

"Go!" screamed Anja, who had been sending more and more snakes to hold the Nightmares at bay. "There are too many!"

Still holding hands, Mirren, Luke and Robyn went thundering up the final steps and tumbled through the door into another dark place. Anja came next. Behind her, the shadows of the chasing creatures fell on the flame-lit walls of the Room of Secrets. The Nightmares' hissing and gargling was becoming deafening, and just as it seemed they'd burst through and attack, Anja slammed the door shut, and with a flash the doorway vanished.

After that, only darkness, and the sounds of their frightened breathing.

CHAPTER 18
A MISTAKE

St Andrews, Scotland, 1999

Susan Anderson sat at the window of her bedroom in the student flat she shared with two other young women, watching the evening rain lash down on the pretty streets of St Andrews. On the desk in front of her, among the scattered sheets of printed research notes and diagrams of planetary orbits, lay the letter she was writing to her parents.

Dear Mum and Dad,
How are you both? Are you missing your brilliant daughter? I know writing an actual letter on actual paper is a bit old-fashioned these days,

but I also know Dad can't work his computer and would probably delete my email before he even opened it, so here we are. Besides, I wanted to send you a picture of me with my friends at the bookshop here in St Andrews.

She stopped writing to glance at the photograph on her desk beside the letter, in which she and two of her friends were holding copies of a paperback book, their thumbs raised in approval and mad looks of happiness on their faces. On the cover there was an illustration of a bare tree, and from the branches hung the titles of the poems inside. The title of the book was *A Piece of My Soul: A Collection of Poems by Charles Anderson.*

She continued to write:

I can't believe you finally have a real book out, Dad! I'm so proud! I've been forcing all my friends to buy copies for their families for Christmas. I should be on commission (ha ha!).

I hope you're both settling into the new house. I can't wait to see it in a few weeks when I come for Christmas. I'm looking forward to exploring Bristol and seeing the school Dad is teaching at now.

I'm pretty gutted that Kevin can't come back from Canada for Christmas. It's really hard having a boyfriend studying so far away. We really miss each other – but he's promised to come and visit me in January!

She stopped writing again; something made her look out of the window, across the street. It was the beginning of December and the rain was pelting down, but that hadn't stopped the Christmas shoppers, who were all hurrying around with umbrellas under the rain-blurred Christmas lights.

Susan stood up. She edged around her desk, pressed her nose to the window. She inhaled sharply, turned around, grabbed her coat and hurried out of her room.

"You going out?" called one of her flatmates from the living room. "Can you get milk?"

"Sure," she said, not really listening. And then she was down the close stairs and out into the torrent, yanking her hood up over her head. She dashed across the street towards the faded golden sign and bundled through the door, where a familiar, faraway quiet enveloped her.

"Hello? Daniel?"

The sound of footsteps, and through the curtain he came, only slightly older than last time she'd seen him. The age gap between them was ever widening; Susan had overtaken him by some years now. She was eighteen, and he was still barely a teenager.

"Hello, Susie."

She rushed towards him but slowed as she got close. "Daniel, are you OK? You look…"

"Terrible?" said Daniel. "Hellish? Awful? Like death warmed up?"

"Well… yeah. Are you ill?"

He waved the question away, but she could not help thinking that something was very wrong. He was pale and thin, and his skin seemed waxy. There were dark circles under his eyes, and a tiredness in those eyes that she had only ever seen in people very much older.

"I'm fine. How are you? Blimey, what age are you now?"

"Eighteen."

"And you're at university here in St Andrews?"

She nodded proudly. "That's right. I'm studying physics and astronomy."

"Good for you." He was staring at her.

"What?" she said, feeling self-conscious.

Daniel blushed a little. "Oh… I just can't believe how grown up you are these days. How long has it been since we saw each other, d'you think?"

"A couple of years," said Susan.

"Really? That long? I'm sorry I haven't been in touch more, Susie. I've just…" He stopped, and she thought she saw a haunted look in his eyes, but it was gone in a moment. "I've been so busy."

"That's OK. Me too. And it's Susan now."

"What is?"

"My name. I prefer Susan."

He considered this. "Oh. Right. No problem."

"Sooo…" said Susan. "What's the occasion, eh?"

"What d'you mean?"

"Why have you come to see me? Not that I'm not happy. But usually you show up on my birthdays and stuff."

"I just missed you, I guess," said Daniel. He let out a wide, long yawn, and his eyes began to roll shut.

"Daniel?" She dashed forward, caught him just as he was about to fall, helped him back to his desk chair. "You need to get to a hospital."

"No, I don't! I'm fine."

"Daniel, look at the state of you! You are far from fine. And as sweet as it was for you to say you came because you miss me, I don't think that's the only reason. What's going on? Daniel?"

But he had fallen into a deep, deep sleep. She shook him a few times, and when it became obvious that he was not going to wake, she made sure he was comfortable in his chair and stood over him. Poor thing. He was obviously exhausted. He did say he'd been busy. She decided to stay in the Emporium for a few hours, until he woke.

Her eyes were drawn towards the curtain, and her mind to the Wonders beyond. Daniel wouldn't mind, would he, if she did a little exploring on her own?

She was a grown-up now, after all. And there was no point in hanging about here listening to him snore like an elephant with a head cold.

And so, with anticipation fluttering in her stomach, she went to the curtain and pushed through.

The first thing she felt was shock.

The Carnival of Wonders, always so vibrant and colourful, had fallen into disrepair. Everywhere she looked, Susan saw tents leaning haphazardly, their material tattered and stained. The alleyways and boulevards between the tents, normally filled with vendors and stalls, were sparsely populated – and those performers who remained were subdued.

As she walked, the ball of dread in her stomach grew heavier, colder.

And then she saw something that she recognised at once, something that she'd seen years ago but the memory of it had been lying dormant until now.

A small white tent of plain canvas, the name on its signpost scratched away.

Inside she found the empty attic room, and the locked door, and she remembered…

"Hello? Are you still there?"

She expected no answer.

"Hello, Susan," came the deep voice, smooth as honey. "How are you?"

"How can you ask about me," said Susan, "when he's keeping you in there?"

"When you have as much time to think as I do," said the man, "you tend to develop a different outlook. You are troubled. I can sense it. What's wrong?"

"Daniel's acting strangely. And his carnival is falling apart. I'm worried about him." She shook her head. "But I guess he's the last person you want to hear about, isn't he? I can understand that."

"On the contrary. I am very interested to hear about our mutual friend. What is wrong with him?"

"I'm not sure. He seems really tired. And he looks… not old – how could he when he barely ages? But… there's something different in his eyes."

"That is worrying," said the man.

Susan frowned. "You're worried about Daniel?"

"Oh, not him. It's the Emporium I'm worried about. I'm stuck in here. If the ship goes down, Susan, I go with it, if you see what I mean."

"Yes," said Susan. She bit her lip, and her gaze danced around the room as she considered. "What if… do you suppose I might be able to let you out?"

A long, long pause.

"I don't doubt that you could do it," said the voice. "But I don't think that you should. You'd make Mr Holmes very angry – and I know what he's capable of."

"But nobody should be trapped like this. It's not right. I'm not naive enough to believe that he's entirely to blame, but whatever your argument was about, surely you could sort it by now?"

"You are a very wise young woman," said the man from the other side of the door. "Alas, I feel that the time is not right. Not yet. If Mr Holmes is having trouble of some sort, the last thing he will wish to consider is me. No, if I were you, I would set about helping him."

Susan frowned. "How?"

"Well, it seems, from what I understand, you have great power, a real connection with this place. If you were to… get your hands on the *Book of Wonders*, for instance… maybe you could recharge the Emporium from your own imagination?"

"You think I should touch the book without permission?"

"You sound like a child," said the voice. "But you're not a child any more, Susan. You are a woman. You are a student of science, of physics and astronomy, and you wish to change the world. I think you are capable of deciding what is right and wrong, don't you? And I fail to see what could possibly be wrong with helping your friend when he is in need."

Fifteen minutes later, Susan was back in the front of the shop. Daniel was still out cold, snoring in loud snorts. She knew he kept the *Book of Wonders* in a drawer in the desk, and her heart battered the inside of her chest as she reached for the handle.

The drawer was locked, but she was amazed to find that the lock clicked open at her touch. She pulled the drawer out and stared down at the book.

Part of her wanted to shut the drawer and forget it. But the man behind the door had been right: she had power, and she was trying to do some good.

Trembling a little, she lifted out the *Book of Wonders*. It was warm in her hands and, as she held it, the power of it coursed through her. Holding that book was like being very hungry, starving, and finally feeling food in your belly. It felt good. Right. The leather cover began to quiver, and glow, and grow warm, and where it had become faded and cracked, the ragged parts smoothed out once more. The book juddered more violently, until Susan's entire body was shaking.

"OK," she said, scared now, "that's enough!"

But the *Book of Wonders* was not done. It shook, and glowed, and became burning hot. The light was fiercely bright; it filled the entire shop.

"Stop!" cried Susan. "Stop!"

And then the *Book of Wonders* was out of her hands, the heat and light gone, the book tumbling through the air, landing on the dusty floorboards.

"What were you thinking?"

Daniel was awake, standing across the shop, a look of fury etched on his face.

"Daniel…" Susan felt like a small child again, like her dad had caught her stealing sweets from the drawer in the kitchen. "Listen, I was…"

"You could have hurt yourself!"

"Oh, come on. I'm fine."

"Yeah, you are. Because I saved you! What if I hadn't woken up? Don't you get it? You might have done some real damage to the Emporium."

"Daniel, I'm sorry. I was trying to help."

"Help? Why?"

Susan threw her arms up. "Look at you! You're exhausted. And the carnival is falling apart. I thought I could give it all a boost."

"The Emporium is connected to me," said Daniel, still half-shouting, "not you."

"You're frightened!" The words left Susan's mouth before she could really think about what she was saying, and there was no putting them back.

"What?" said Daniel, screwing up his face. "What are you talking about?"

Susan was angry now, angry that her friend was treating her this way when she'd been trying to come to his aid. "You're frightened of me, aren't you?" Her voice was very low. "I can see it in your face. It's the same look Mum and Dad get whenever I try to speak to them about my… my magic. I thought you understood."

"I do," said Daniel. "Of course I do."

"You don't. The only person who ever understood was my grandad." She blinked tears away. "He wasn't frightened of me."

Daniel looked like he'd been punched in the gut. "Susie, I know you were trying to help, but there are other things going on here." He looked past her, seemingly into the distance of his own thoughts.

"Then let me help."

"No."

"Why not?"

"I don't need help."

"But Daniel, I could maybe—"

"I said I DON'T NEED HELP!" When he shouted, the *Book of Wonders* leapt into the air and crashed back down with a thump. The cover crackled with magical static. Daniel leaned over his desk and slumped into his chair, breathless. "Leave me alone. Please."

Susan nodded, and turned away, and left the shop without saying another word.

CHAPTER 19

OFF THE TRACKS

The Nowhere Emporium, Present Day

"I can't see anything!"

"Do not panic."

"Aoow! Who put their finger in my eye? Someone just put their finger in my eye!"

"Well don't stand so close then!"

"Where are we?"

"I wish we had some light!"

No sooner had those words escaped Luke's mouth than the compass, nestled safely in his palm, began to emit a cold silver-blue light that filled the darkness, casting a ghostly glow on their surroundings: damp rock walls and a low rock ceiling.

"We're in a tunnel," he said.

"Wow." Robyn was feigning wonder. "You're right, Luke! I'd never have picked up on that!"

"I know you're joking," Luke shot back, "but somehow I believe you."

"You two," said Mirren, "shut it."

"The door has taken us into another Wonder," said Anja, ignoring the bickering. "But I don't think I've ever seen this one. There are so many, you see."

"At least it didn't lead us back out to the corridors this time," said Robyn.

Mirren's mouth was dry, her voice a little croaky. "He'll find us again, won't he? He'll send those things after us." She imagined running through these suffocating tunnels, the awful sounds of the Nightmares on her tail.

"When he does," said Robyn, "I dunno if the key will be much use next time." She held it up in the light of the compass; it had rusted right through, and small fragments of it were flaking off and twirling down to the rock floor.

"He'll find us," said Anja grimly. "I have no doubt. But the Emporium is unimaginably vast, so I hope we'll have a little time."

Mirren nodded. "Then we should make the most of it. Which way, Luke?"

He consulted the compass, pointed off to the right. They walked, which was a more difficult task than it might sound, because the floor of the tunnel was uneven, and even by the strong silvery light of the compass it was easy to miss dips and bumps in the path. The compass led them on and on, turn after turn after turn, until they had lost all sense of direction. The underground air was damp and thick and heavy. It made them breathless.

After a while they began to notice sturdy wooden supports framing the tunnel walls.

"It's a mine," said Robyn.

"It is?"

"Yeah, I think so. I've seen places like this in the old cowboy movies my dad likes to watch when he's at home. They call 'em spaghetti westerns. Know why?" When nobody answered, she went on. "It's because they were mostly filmed in Italy – not in the Old West like they want you to think. Italy... Spaghetti... Get it?"

"Wait," said Anja. "What's that up ahead?" She slowed and signalled for them to hang back, then crept forward until they could barely make her out at all. "It's OK," came the call. "In fact, I think it's good. Come!"

As they walked, the light of the compass pushed back the dark until they saw the beginnings of what seemed to be a small railway track on the ground. On the track sat a metal cart, like a very deep, square bathtub.

Luke held out the compass. "It's pointing right at the cart."

"D'you think it's safe?" Robyn was examining the cart with a very doubtful look on her face.

Mirren rolled her eyes. "Oh yes! I'm sure health and safety have been all over this place. Come on!" Trying to act much braver than she really felt, Mirren climbed into the cart. Next came Luke, then Anja. "Are you coming?" she said to Robyn. "Or do you want to stay and be the welcome party for whatever new horror Sharpe sends after us this time?"

Her words seemed to do the trick; Robyn leapt into the cart like a shot.

"What now?" asked Luke.

Robyn leaned over the side. "Well, in the movies there's always a pump-handle thingy that makes it go along the track. But I can't see anything like thaaaaaAAAAA—"

Without anyone touching it, without anyone doing anything at all, the cart shot forward. In seconds they were travelling at such a speed Mirren thought her face was going to peel off. It was like being on the world's most insane rollercoaster; the cart was almost flying, screaming around corners and climbing steeply and dropping down again as the tunnels rose and fell, its wheels screeching and moaning and sparking on the tracks.

Mirren would have screamed too, if it had been possible to get enough air into her lungs. As it was, she could only grip the side of the cart and hope that it would stop before it went careering off into oblivion.

And then the roar of the cart was overcome by another sound, a huge explosion from behind them, and the tunnel filled with angry orange light and intense heat. Still hanging on for her life, Mirren twisted around to see, and this time she found the air in her lungs to scream.

A wall of fire was tearing after them through the tunnel. As it came nearer, the flames took the shape of a dragon's head, its fiery tongue lashing at the air, and Vindictus Sharpe's terrible, maniacal laughter rang out just as it had in the throne room.

The cart screamed onward, up and down, left and right, wheels barely on the tracks, and with every second that passed, the fire drew nearer, the heat more intense. It was almost upon them now. Mirren was sure that this was the end, that she would die down here in the darkness. That she'd never see Mum again.

The cart shot out of the tunnel and into an enormous rock chamber. There was no floor here; the track was built upon a rickety wooden frame that seemed to stretch forever down into the gloom. And from the tunnel followed the fire dragon, enormous, roaring and lashing and biting at them.

As the cart reached the centre of this great ravine, it tipped sideward with a sudden jolt, sending Mirren and her friends tumbling down, down, down, as the pitch-black hurtled past them.

Splash!

The shock of deep, cold water on Mirren's flesh, soaking her clothes, her hair.

Blackness.

Then the water lit up, and Mirren stared up at the surface, which was momentarily alive and dancing with wildfire, before all was dark and silent again.

She swam for the surface, gasping when her head broke through. Mum had taken her to swimming lessons when she was tiny, determined that Mirren believe from a young age that she could learn to do things just as well as anyone else. She was a natural in the water; she'd spent so much time in the local pool that using her legs and one arm to tread water had become second nature. She was a stronger swimmer than almost anyone she knew.

"Luke?" she yelled. "Robyn? Anja?"

Splashing from nearby, and then Robyn's voice. "Mirren? Mirren, where are you?"

"I'm here!"

Anja called from the black. "Are you all OK?"

They found each other, the three of them. But…

"Luke. Where is he?" Mirren's chest filled with dread. "Luke? Luke!"

A faint glow nearby caught her eye, and she swam a fast crawl towards it, her little arm angled constantly into the water while her legs kicked and her right arm carved through the water with large, circular motions. "Luke!" He was under the water; she could see him down there, five metres or so.

She dived down and realised at once that his pyjamas were snagged on the rock wall. He was pulling and kicking desperately, and when he saw her, he waved and shook his head, bubbles spilling from his nose and mouth. Mirren swam to him, grabbed his arm, and nodded reassurance. He held the compass out so that she might see better by its glow, and she reached out and worked the material of his pyjama bottoms free. Then they were swimming for the surface again, and glorious cold air filled Mirren's lungs, and she heard Luke spluttering, gasping, breathing. He was OK.

Anja swam towards them, moving as easily in the water as a mermaid. Robyn followed; she was not quite as graceful a swimmer, using a cross between breaststroke and doggy paddle. "You alright, Luke?" she asked.

"Yeah," he said, wheezing a bit. "Thanks to Mirren. I'd have been a goner if you hadn't found me."

"You'd have done the same, right?" said Mirren. But rather than answer, Luke swam over and hugged her. "I'll never forget it," he whispered.

Anja was now floating serenely on her back. "Is the compass still working?"

Luke opened his hand. The compass was dripping wet, but still emitting its strong silvery light. The dial was resolute in pointing the way. "I think it's fine."

"Then we swim."

They moved through a maze of flooded tunnels, following the compass dial as it swung around, stopping here and there to rest where it was possible to grab crags of rock. Mirren could not help imagining that something else would come after them. They were safe from fire here, of course, but her mind insisted on playing tricks on her, telling her that some creature was swimming beneath them, ready to pull them under.

At last, the water became shallow enough to wade, and the level continued to drop until they were walking in only a few inches of it, and then, finally, none at all.

Robyn twitched her nose. "You smell that?"

Mirren took a breath. "Yeah. It's fresh air! Smells like the seaside!"

They hurried on through the twisting caves and turned a final corner to discover a wide opening, which led to a pebbly beach and a small cove surrounded by high chalk cliffs. The night sky was like crystal, scattered with twinkling stars and constellations. Warm air brushed their faces, and the sound of the gentle sea was calming.

Mirren felt Anja brush past her, watched as she strode to the place where the sea met the sand and gazed out at the water. Mirren wondered what had caught Anja's attention, and then she saw. Out beyond the cove, a handsome pirate ship with tall masts came drifting into view. Oil lamps twinkled all over the ship, and its huge sails billowed in the breeze. It was a fine sight. But the finest sight of all was the flag flying atop the highest mast. It carried a symbol Mirren and her friends had come to know very well: an open book.

Anja turned around, her face breaking into a wide smile. "I did not recognise the caves we came through, but it turns out I *have* been to this Wonder before. I know it very well, in fact. Oh, that compass is a clever thing indeed! It has brought us to the last stronghold of the League of the Book."

CHAPTER 20
MOVING ON

Maternity Ward, Southern General Hospital, Glasgow, 2009

As Susan Feather lay in the hospital bed and watched her new baby daughter sleep peacefully, she wondered if it was possible to be any happier.

Little Mirren had arrived two days before. She had decided to come three weeks early, and the birth had been by emergency C-section, but when she finally appeared in the world, there had never been a more perfect baby.

Kevin had bought an enormous teddy to herald his daughter's arrival, and it sat at the end of the bed, beside a dozen cards congratulating the happy couple on their new addition. Susan's mum and dad had rushed all the way up from Bristol, and Kevin's mum was flying over from Canada the following week. This was all lovely, and she was very glad that she was surrounded by a loving family. But above all else, Susan treasured the times she had her daughter all to herself, when it was just the two of them, like now.

Mirren woke up and began to make agitated sounds. Susan hurried over, lifted her from the cot and hugged her, this perfect little miracle.

"Quiet now, sunshine girl. That's it. I'm here. Let's go for a little walk, eh?"

Susan walked around the ward for a while, saying hello to the midwives and nurses who were on duty – some of whom had helped deliver Mirren. When Mirren had settled once more, Susan headed back to the room she shared with three other new mothers. As she reached the doorway, she stopped, and took a sharp breath. She stared at the end of her bed.

Someone had tied seven black and gold balloons to the bedframe, and they sparkled and twinkled as they gently spun on their sleek black ribbons.

Only one of the other mothers was awake.

"Did you see who brought these new balloons in?" Susan asked her.

The woman, who was feeding her newborn son, looked up, frowned in a puzzled sort of way. "I thought they'd always been there, Susan. No?"

Susan forced a smile. "I must be more exhausted than I thought." She turned and placed the sleeping little Mirren back in her cot.

When she straightened up, she saw the gift. It lay on the bed, a small cube wrapped in the most expensive-looking black wrapping paper she'd ever seen, tied with a shining golden ribbon. Sitting on the edge of the bed, she picked up the gift and unwrapped it, her hands trembling so much she could barely untie the bow.

Inside the box, sitting in a nest of black tissue paper, was a snow globe. Susan took the snow globe from the box and examined it. It rested on an ornately carved base of stained black wood, and the glass of the dome was so fine that it seemed impossibly fragile. Inside the globe was the perfect model of a miniature street, with a row of shops. And there, in the centre of the row, sat the Nowhere Emporium.

As Susan brought the snow globe closer, tears spilled from her eyes, and she wiped them away so that she could properly see. She shook the globe, making the snow fall on the miniature street. Then the tiny door of the Emporium opened, and a flock of white doves burst from the shop. They flew up and up, flew through the glass, escaping the snow globe, one of them landing on Susan's hand.

A voice, Daniel's voice, spoke clearly to her. "You are always welcome in the Nowhere Emporium,

Susan. Maybe one day I'll get to meet Mirren. Congratulations. I know you'll be a great mum."

The tears came again, and this time she let them. She had not been to the Nowhere Emporium for years, had not thought about it at all recently; there were more important things to worry about, like work and becoming a parent. Thinking about it tonight opened a door to her past, let in memories of Grandad, and her parents, and her childhood. She remembered the magic in her, the power she'd tried to ignore as she'd grown, pushed back deep down inside. She had kept it a secret from her friends, even from her husband.

She heard Kevin's voice along the corridor and woke from her memories. Packing the snow globe away, she slid the box under her bed.

"Whoa!" said her husband in a loud whisper. He pointed to the new balloons. "Who sent these?" He leaned over and kissed her.

"Just an old friend from uni," she said, trying to sound breezy.

"That's nice. But black and gold? For a baby? Bit unusual, eh?"

Susan managed a small laugh. "I guess some people are just different."

"Yes, they are." Kevin had already forgotten the balloons and fallen under the spell of his new daughter again.

Susan watched her family, and smiled, and thought that life was good.

Two days later, when Susan had gone home, one of the ward cleaners found a black gift box under the bed. Inside the box was a beautiful snow globe. The cleaner asked around, but nobody knew who it belonged to. When no one claimed it, the snow globe became a decoration at the nurse's station, and there it sits to this day.

CHAPTER 21
A PIRATES' FEAST

The Nowhere Emporium, Present Day

The ship sent out a rescue boat, and soon Mirren and her friends were aboard the main vessel – the *Crescent Queen*. The crew, a band of pirates a hundred strong, looked as if they'd spilled directly from the pages of an adventure book, which Mirren supposed they had, in a way. They came from the *Book of Wonders*, after all. The pirates, with tattoos and cutlasses and weathered, leathery skin, wearing big-buckled belts and eyeliner, gave them a raucous welcome, singing and cheering, hoisting Anja shoulder-high and chanting her name.

"Unhand her, boys!" The door to the cabin burst open, and there stood a tall man with long sandy hair hanging over his handsome, bearded face. He wore black velvet breeches and waistcoat, with a gold silken shirt and a broad leather sash. One of his legs was missing from the knee down, and in its place was a shining silver peg studded with rubies. His cheeks were ruddy, his eyes sparkling blue, and when they settled on Anja, they lit up. He laughed and hobbled towards her, shaking her madly by the hand. "Anja! 'Ow wonderful it is to lay eyes on you!"

"Good to see you, Jean. Very good indeed."

"Where 'ave you been?" said the pirate. He spoke with a slight French accent. "We all thought—"

"That Sharpe had turned me into a Nightmare? Almost. But then years ago I found my way to a lost fragment of Daniel's carnival. It is good to be back."

The pirate looked around at Mirren, Robyn and Luke. "Ahoy! Who are your friends, dear Anja?"

Anja introduced them.

"I am Jean Reynard." The pirate offered handshakes all round. "Any friend of Daniel Holmes is a friend of mine. He created me, you know. We are all but inky markings on the pages of his great book, yes?" He laughed, and then became very serious, distracted, and turned his face to the sky. "The wind 'as changed. I fear we will not be alone for much longer." He began to bark at his crew. "Come about, you dogs! Weigh anchor and let us go! *Allons-y!*" His words sent huge men scurrying away like rats. "Set a course for the edge of the world!" Reynard yelled at the top of his lungs, bringing another chorus of cheers. The air filled with sea shanties as his men worked to ready the ship for the journey, and soon the *Crescent Queen* had swung around and was cutting through the vast sea like a blade, salt spray washing over Mirren and her companions.

When Mirren, Luke and Robyn were warm and dry, Reynard took them to the table in his quarters, which were grand and gaudy and draped in fine tapestries. The cook served up a feast of roast beef and potatoes, chicken legs and exotic spiced couscous jewelled with pomegranate. Mirren ate and ate until she thought her stomach was going to explode. It was the finest food she'd ever tasted, better even than Mum's spag bol.

Mum.

Her face flashed bright in Mirren's mind, and a cold wave of sadness broke over her heart. She excused herself from the table and went to get some air.

Back on deck, she stood at the gunwale and gazed out over the endless dark expanse of ocean. The moon was high in a clear sky, and the stars were so numerous and bright that you could almost imagine the sound of their twinkling rays. "Are you out there somewhere, Mum?" Mirren whispered.

"She is, *mon amie.*" Reynard had come up on deck too. "May I join you?"

"Of course."

His silver leg *click-clacked* on the deck. He leaned on the gunwale beside her. "I know it can be tough to answer such questions, but tell me, if it is not too personal… has your arm always been that way?"

"No. I was in a car crash when I was a baby."

"Car? *Oui*, I have seen those in some of the other Wonders. Pah! Noisy, dirty machines! This is the way to travel." He swept his arm across the vast night sky.

"What about you?" Mirren asked, indicating his leg.

He smiled. "*Moi?* I lost my leg in a struggle with a mighty kraken in these very waters! The beast banished twelve of my crew to Davy Jones's Locker – and almost took the *Crescent Queen* too! But I 'ave a trick or three up my sleeve, yes?" He gazed out across the water. The full moon reflected on the tumbling waves, scattering silver all across the horizon. "He is still out there, that monster. One day I will find him again. It is… 'ow do you say… my purpose. My reason for being. I will find him. Just like you will find your mother."

"How can everyone be so sure of that?" Mirren dabbed her tear-brimmed eyes. "What if I *can't* find her? Or what if I do find her, but I can't help?"

Reynard turned to face her, leaning with one arm on the edge of the ship. "I 'ave known you only a handful of hours, *mon amie*, and yet I can already tell that you 'ave fire in your heart. The way your friends speak of you… the way they look at you… you are their *leader*."

"But I've never been anyone's leader. I don't know how."

Jean Reynard smiled. "In the beginning, no one knows 'ow. But you will learn."

"You really think they see me that way?"

"I do not think – I know. They would follow you anywhere, just as my crew would follow me into the very jaws of the kraken!" He straightened up. "And now you must rest, yes? You are exhausted. Come. I will find you and your friends a place to sleep."

Mirren did not argue. A deep tiredness had seeped into her bones.

Reynard lead them to the belly of the ship, which smelled of rum and old vegetables. Here they climbed into the waiting comfort of hammocks, which swung gently back and forth with the motion of the *Crescent Queen* as she rose and fell with the waves.

Mirren was asleep almost at once, Mum's snow globe clutched to her chest. She dreamed of a fountain, and a black tower, and a pair of icy blue eyes.

CHAPTER 22

LOST

Bristol, 2012

Susan sat in the living room of her parents' house in Bristol, curled up under a blanket on the couch. A mug of forgotten hot chocolate sat on the coffee table. She was looking at the television, but if anyone had asked her about the programme that was on, she wouldn't have been able to tell them a single thing.

Her mind, as had been the case almost every moment of every day since the accident, could think of nothing but her wee girl, how her life would be changed forever by the injuries she'd suffered in the crash. How she'd never know her daddy.

A crackle over the baby monitor, and then the

staticky sound of Mirren's little voice. "Mummy?"

Susan got up stiffly and went upstairs as quietly as she could manage, passing the bedroom where her parents slept soundly, and into Mirren's room. She found the child fast asleep, looking peaceful. She must have called out from a dream. Susan gently kissed her daughter on the cheek and went back downstairs to turn off the TV.

Tap tap.

Susan flicked the TV switch off.

Tap tapetty tap.

She straightened up, massaging her lower back, which was still painful from the accident. The sound was coming from the window. She stood up, and as she approached the drawn curtains, the gentle tapping went on. It sounded, she thought, like an insect, a moth maybe.

When she opened the curtains there was no moth. There was a feather. A pure white feather, floating in the air. Susan stared. She blinked. She began to wonder if she was still dreaming.

Without thinking about it, she flicked a hand; the latch clicked, and the window swung open. It was the first time she'd used magic in years, and she was shocked to find that she could still do it. She was also shocked to find that it felt good. It had been so long since anything had felt good – besides holding Mirren – since Kevin died.

The feather drifted in through the open window. Susan held out a hand, and the feather twirled into her open palm. It was ice-cold, and pure white, and perfect.

It took off again after a long moment, and swirled up and around her head, and she watched it drift back out of the window again, where it stopped and hung in place. A thought: did the feather want her to follow? Could a feather *want* anything?

And then, as she stared, something beyond the feather caught her eye, something across the cul-de-sac: glistening black brickwork.

Her breath caught in her throat and her heart began to race. Before she knew what she was doing, Susan was out in the hall, fetching a jacket from the cupboard under the stairs, slipping it on over her comfortable sweater and jogging bottoms.

As quietly as she could manage, Susan opened the front door, stepped out into the night, and locked it behind her again. The pure white feather twirled through the darkness, led her down the garden path, out the gate, across the street, walking slowly all the while towards a place she had almost forgotten, a place she had been sure she would never revisit.

And yet, here it was, exactly as it always had been.

The Nowhere Emporium.

The feather hung in front of the doorway. Susan came closer, and as she approached, the door swung open, familiar and bewitching scents ensnaring her, pulling her in to the dim beyond. She entered. The door closed gently behind her, leaving her alone in the shop – and she was alone; this time there was no Daniel behind his desk. The feather had come in too; it floated towards the curtain, and she followed.

"Daniel?" The sound of her own voice was somewhat surprising; she had used it less and less since the accident, and it was weak and croaky. "Are you here?"

No answer. Susan pushed through the curtain to the Carnival of Wonders.

She looked around, puzzled and disappointed at how ramshackle the place had become. Many of the tents seemed on the verge of collapse, their once colourful canvas walls faded and dirty and torn. There was no sign of any of the performers or vendors. The twilight sky, which had, she remembered, been a glorious wash of golds and reds and purples, was now a dull and dirty grey. The air itself was heavy with a dust of ashy particles, which made her cough and sneeze.

"Daniel, where are you?"

Still no answer. A few feet away, the feather bobbed in a way that let Susan know it was getting impatient, and she followed it again as it streaked away, through the maze of faded tents, until she arrived at a black canvas tent she remembered very well indeed.

It was the first Wonder she'd ever written in the book.

The pure white feather floated serenely down to the ground at the entranceway to the tent, and there it faded and disappeared. Susan stared at the spot on the ground where the feather had been, and then she blinked, and looked up, and pushed through the golden curtain.

She was back in the long grass on the banks of a lazy river. The sky was vast and heavy with dark clouds, the surrounding grass fields dotted with oak and chestnut trees. She had only been here once before, and yet it was so familiar that she knew every part of it. Of course she did. It had come from her imagination, after all.

When the rain began to fall, she instinctively looked around for a place to shelter. But as the drops landed on her, she stopped looking around and looked up instead. Slowly, as the pattering raindrops became a drum, and then a downpour, Susan did something she hadn't done since the car crash.

She smiled.

Happiness. Drops of happiness were falling from the sky. Her mind had been lost in a dark fog for so long that she had almost forgotten how to be happy. But every droplet was cutting through that fog. Warm thoughts filled her head, happy memories of her husband and the time they had spent together. How she'd laughed at his corny jokes. How he'd leave Post-it notes hidden around the house for her to find, each with a loving little message scribbled on it. How happy they had been when Mirren was born, and how frightened and content and excited they'd been to take her home from the hospital for the first time, to start their life together as a proper family.

The rain – the happiness – continued to fall.

Susan thought of her parents, of the love and support they'd always shown her. She thought of Grandad, and the tears in her eyes now were not of sadness or grief or anger, but of love and thankfulness. And Mirren. The thought of her little girl was the brightest light of all, shining in her mind like a newborn star.

The rain stopped.

Susan stood on the riverbank, dabbing at her eyes. When she left the tent and was back in the run-down Carnival of Wonders, she looked all about, tears still glistening in her eyes like jewels, and said, "Thank you, Daniel. Thank you so much."

Far away, in another tent, an old-fashioned painted wagon sat in a field in a pretty meadow surrounded by forest and mountains.

Inside the wagon, Daniel Holmes lay on his comfortable bed, eyes shut, the *Book of Wonders* open on his chest. In his mind's eye he was watching Susan.

He was so tired. The Emporium was a heavy weight around his neck, and it was getting heavier. Something was very wrong. He had felt that for a while. It was as if some poison was pumping through the veins of the place, spreading. He was worried he would lose control. Worried he was not strong enough to continue.

It had taken most of his strength to send the feather to guide Susan back to her Raining Happiness Wonder. He was exhausted, but oh how it had been worth it to see her smile, to feel the darkness around her heart thin.

She'll be fine, he thought.

And, knowing this to be true, he closed his eyes and fell asleep.

When she left the Raining Happiness tent, Susan thought about looking for Daniel. He had helped her so much this night; she would have loved nothing more than to hug him and tell him how much it meant. But it was obvious that he did not want her to find him, that he did not want to talk – and if Daniel did not want to be found in this place, there was nothing she could do about it.

She was almost back at the red curtain of the shopfront when she stopped, because she saw another tent that she recognised very well, though she was sure it was in a different place from last time.

The tent was small and plain, and she knew what was inside before she went through the entrance. Sure enough, here was the dusty attic room, and the locked door.

"It's all so sad, isn't it?" came the deep voice from the other side.

Susan approached the door. "What?"

A sigh from beyond the door. "That this place will soon be no more."

"What do you mean?"

"Surely you can see?" said the man. "All you have to do is look around the Emporium to know it's on its last legs."

Susan worried her bottom lip. "It's really as bad as you say?"

"Susan," said the voice, 'I have never been surer of anything. Daniel is sick, I think. Or perhaps when Mr Silver handed over the Emporium to him, he overestimated Daniel's power. Whatever it is, it has been eating away at the place for years, like a disease. And, well, I think the end is in sight."

"But we can't let that happen!" said Susan. "We have to do something."

After a long pause, the man on the other side of the door said, "I don't know if there's anything that can be done… Unless…"

"Unless what?"

"No," said the man. "Forget it. It's too dangerous."

"Tell me," said Susan. "I don't care if it's dangerous. Do you know what Daniel did for me tonight? He gave me my smile back, and I won't stand by and watch him lose everything. I'll do anything to help him."

Another pause.

"Are you sure?" said the voice.

"Anything," repeated Susan.

When the voice next spoke, it was soft and low and hungry. "There is one thing."

When he had explained, Susan nodded. "You sure this will work?"

"As sure as I can be, yes."

"If it helps Daniel," she said, "what is there to think about, really?"

And with that, she closed her eyes, and concentrated on the lock on the door. In her mind, she felt it give a little, and a little more, and she applied more pressure, until…

Click.

The door was unlocked.

Susan watched as the handle turned slowly, and with another *click*, swung open.

She tried to see what was on the other side of the doorway, but the blackness was thick as ink.

Slow footsteps, then he emerged from the darkness.

He filled the doorway, big and bearlike, with massive shoulders, a square jaw and neatly cropped silvery hair. His eyes were ice-blue and sharp and intelligent. He wore a suit the colour of the night sky.

Susan was thirty-one years old, but standing in his presence, she felt like a child.

"Hello," she said nervously.

He looked down at her and smiled, but the smile did not put her at ease.

"Hello, Susan. I think, now that we have met properly, it is time you know my name." He made a small bow. "Vindictus Sharpe, at your service." He offered a hand, and it swallowed Susan's when they shook. "Come. There is little time to lose."

Half an hour later, Susan's feet were aching from keeping up with the pace of Sharpe's stride.

"Where is it?" she asked.

"Patience."

"Are you sure you'll be able to find it? You said only Daniel can see it."

"I've been a part of this place for so long, it runs through my veins," he said. "I'll find it, and I think you will be able to see it too. I'm telling—" He stopped, pointed a huge finger, and smiled. "There! What did I tell you!"

Through the entrance, and inside the tent, they stood on the icy surface of a frozen pond. All around, the trees were coated in thick spikes of frost, and the sky was endlessly blue. The air was crisp and smelled of winter. In the centre of the frozen pond were three tiers of circular stone.

Susan walked to the fountain. "And that's the imagination you spoke about? That silvery stuff?"

"Yes. That's it."

"But there's barely a trickle," said Susan. "It's almost dry."

Sharpe nodded gravely. "Yes. It's worse than I imagined." He squeezed one of his hands with the other. "It may be too far gone. We may be too late."

"No." Susan was defiant. "I can do it. I can sort it. I know I can."

Sharpe gave her a doubtful look. "Then you must do so."

That heavy ball of fear was back in Susan's stomach, spinning, lurching. But she thought of her daughter and pushed the fear back down. Holding out an open hand, she closed her eyes and concentrated with everything she had on the *Book of Wonders*, on the connection she felt with it, and with the Emporium. She remembered how it felt in her hands, how the power of it had flowed through her. She thought of the smell of the pages, of the feel of the cracked leather cover.

"OK," she said, talking to the Nowhere Emporium itself. "Take what you need. Take my imagination. Use my power. Do it!"

The ground trembled very slightly, shaking the loose outer coating of dusty frost. Susan felt a warmth bloom deep in her chest, and the heat radiated through her hands and arms and body, until it felt like she was entirely ablaze with magic.

When the heat died away, the trickle of the fountain became a bubbling rush.

Susan opened her eyes. The fountain was overflowing with the silvery liquid of her imagination. She stared at Sharpe, let out a single breath of laughter, and ran for the entranceway.

Outside she found a riot of rich colour, of pristine striped tents and busy performers, and the scents of popcorn and caramel, all under a twilight sky brushed with purple-gold.

"It's back to normal!" she said. "It's really back!"

"No," said Sharpe, who had joined her. "It's better." He offered a hand, and his mouth spread into a wide grin. His teeth were perfect and white. "Well done, Susan. Well done indeed."

Susan returned the smile. Then, feeling fit to burst with a strange, childish pride, she shook his hand.

Susan blinked.

Her head was light, fuzzy – it felt like she had only just awakened from a long, deep sleep, that part of her was still in that strange nowhere between asleep and awake.

She was outside. It was dark and cold. She checked her watch, saw that it was almost one in the morning. Susan had never been known to sleepwalk, but she presumed that's exactly what she'd just been doing. What other explanation could there be for her standing across the cul-de-sac from her parents' house, staring into Mr and Mrs Singh's front room?

There was something else though.

She'd had a dream, hadn't she? Something about a shop? Or magic? What was it? The harder she tried to grasp the fading echo of the dream, the further it slipped away, until nothing at all remained.

She could not be sure what had happened in her sleeping state – only that she had awakened feeling more clear-headed than at any time since the accident, since she'd lost Kevin. She felt different, like she had been in a dark maze, going around and around, and finally found the exit.

Her little girl was asleep in bed. When she woke up, she'd need her mum, and Susan would be there, always.

Shivering, she turned and walked across the street and up the path. Before she shut the door to the dark and cold, she glanced one more time across the street, where the neat houses sat in a perfect row. Nothing unusual. Nothing out of place.

When Susan went inside, she could not shake the feeling that she had forgotten something very important. When she woke up, however, that feeling would be gone.

CHAPTER 23

MAKING FRIENDS

The Nowhere Emporium, Present Day

When she opened her eyes, Mirren first thought she had been dreaming, that she was in her bedroom and she would get out of bed and walk to the kitchen of their flat and see Mum sipping coffee and reading the morning news on her phone. Then she felt the hammock swing gently, and smelled the smells of the ship, and she knew that it was real.

Other than the creak of the ship as it coasted over the waves, there were only two sounds. The first was the rumble of Luke's snoring. This made Mirren smile. The second was soft and would have been easy to miss. It was the sound of someone crying.

She sat up in the hammock, which was not an easy task, and by the light of the lamps she looked over and saw that Robyn had hidden herself away under a blanket, and she was shaking and quivering.

"Robyn?"

A gasp, and Robyn's face appeared over the dirty blanket. Her eyes were puffy and red, her cheeks wet. "Oh," she said with a sniff. "I thought you were asleep."

"What's the matter?"

Robyn glanced over towards Luke's hammock, as if making sure he couldn't hear. "I'm frightened," she said. "I want to go home."

"Me too," said Mirren.

The ship rose and fell rhythmically beneath them, the waves whooshing against the hull.

"Really? You don't seem frightened. You always seem so brave."

Mirren smiled. "I get that from Mum. She's always been good at making out everything's alright."

"What d'you mean?"

"Well... like the times when we don't have much money and I need new clothes. She pretends like it's nothing to worry about, but I can see it in her eyes. Or the days when she catches someone staring at my arm. She pretends it doesn't bother her, but I can see it makes her angry." She rubbed her left arm.

"What actually happened?" asked Robyn in a tentative voice. A short pause. "You don't have to tell me if you don't want to."

"No, it's fine. It's natural to be curious; I'm used to people asking. I really can't remember – I was just a baby – but Mum has told me about it. Dad was driving, and this car came flipping over the barrier from the other side of the motorway and hit us."

Robyn was biting her lip as she listened. "And your dad?"

"He died in hospital later that day. Mum was in the back seat with me, see, and they think that's how we survived."

"I'm so sorry," said Robyn. Mirren was watching her with interest; it was as if she was sorting things out in her mind, arranging her thoughts. "I know what I am, you know."

Mirren frowned. "What d'you mean?"

"Oh, come on," said Robyn. "You know what I mean. I know exactly the type of person I've turned into. I'm a bully. I'm horrible."

Mirren couldn't quite believe what she was hearing. "Robyn… you're not *that* bad."

"Don't lie," said Robyn. "I'm a monster."

"You can be a right pain in the bum sometimes," Mirren admitted. "But I wouldn't say you're a monster."

"Well I would," said Robyn. She was quiet again for a minute. "You know the message this Daniel Holmes guy sent the three of us tonight? The thing that made us come here?"

"Yeah?"

"Yours told you that your mum was in trouble, right?"

"That's right."

"And Luke's…" She glanced over towards him again and lowered her voice. "His message told him that you needed his help. That's why he came."

"That's what he says."

"You know why I came, Mirren? You know what my message said? It said that I should come tonight because it was my chance to finally make some friends."

"What? You've got friends." Mirren pictured the gaggle of girls who always followed Robyn around in school.

"Not real friends. They only hang about with me so I don't pick on them, not because they like me. They never invite me to parties or sleepovers. That's one of the reasons I pick on you and Luke." She paused, trying to find the words. Mirren could tell that Robyn was finding this all very difficult. "I can see that you really are best friends. You care about each other. And it makes me jealous because I want that. I walk around showing off my new trainers and fancy phone and I make fun of you and Luke for not having much, but you know what? The only reason I get all that stuff is because my dad feels guilty for being away on business so much.

He's barely home at all, and when he is, he's got paperwork or phone calls to take. I know that's nothing compared with what you've been through, but I just wanted you to know... Oh, I don't know what I'm trying to say!"

Mirren sat in the hammock, staring across at Robyn. When the night began, she could never have imagined that they'd be talking in this way. In spite of herself, Mirren was beginning to warm to her. "I think I understand," she said at last.

Robyn wiped her eyes again. "You do?"

"Yeah. You're right: I have been through a lot, but that doesn't mean I can't listen to other people's problems, or that you should feel bad about telling me what's going on with you, you know? Friends support each other."

"Friends? Will you give me another chance?"

Mirren considered this. She nodded. "I will. But do me a favour. If we ever get out of here, don't go back to your old ways, will you?"

"I won't," said Robyn solemnly. "This place has really shown me what's important. I just want to get home and see my mum and dad, and my brother. I promise I'll change."

"Well, all right then," said Mirren.

"What about Luke?" said Robyn in that low voice again. "You think he'll give me a chance too?"

"If there's one thing for certain about Luke," said

Mirren, "it's that he forgives people too easily. I think you'll be fine."

Robyn nodded and lay back down in her hammock, and Mirren did the same. She stared up at nothing in particular and smiled to herself. Well, that was a turn-up for the books, wasn't it? Robyn Prince apologising to her. Anything really could happen in this place.

The ship rocked up and down, and Mirren pictured the vast ocean reflecting the moon and the twinkling stars. There were definitely worse ways to travel than this.

CHAPTER 24
AN OLD ENEMY

The Nowhere Emporium, Sometime After
Susan Feather's Last Visit

Daniel walked the passageways of the great Carnival of Wonders, noting all the places where there were problems. The tents had been degrading for some time, some of the Wonders within warping, and as a result he was having to close more and more tents down.

"You *must* bring in an apprentice to help you." Caleb was walking with him, shaking his head. "We cannot go on like this."

"I know that," said Daniel.

"Then you know what you have to do. Bring her back."

Daniel stopped, brushed his red hair from his eyes. "Susan has moved on, Caleb. She has a family now, a child to look after. I can't ask her to take this on."

"And what is the alternative, hmm? Let the place continue to go to the dogs? You are close to crumbling yourself. Please, Daniel, ask her."

Daniel looked up into the eyes of his most trusted member of staff. Was Caleb right? In all the world, Daniel could think of no one else who could help him as well as Susan Feather. But so much had changed, so much time had passed...

"Oh, I wouldn't trust her if I were you."

Daniel peered around, wondering where the voice had come from. "Who's there? Who said that?" His eyes fixed on a little tent of plain, tattered canvas. He had seen it only once before – the first time anything he'd written in the *Book of Wonders* had gone wrong.

"An old friend," came the voice again. It was deep and smooth and familiar.

"Show yourself." Daniel tried to steady his shaking hands.

"If you say so. I have waited long enough for this moment."

The entranceway to the tent rippled. Daniel took a sharp breath, clutched the *Book of Wonders* to his chest. He could not believe what he was seeing. Striding through the curtain, as if stepping from one of Daniel Holmes's nightmares, was the greatest enemy he had ever faced. "I-I don't believe it. It's impossible!"

Vindictus Sharpe stood tall and bearlike, his neat silver hair glistening, his smile like a knife. "Haven't you learned by now, Daniel, that nothing is impossible in the Nowhere Emporium?"

Caleb left Daniel's side, rushed at Sharpe.

"Caleb, no!"

But too late. With a lazy flick of the hand, Sharpe sent Caleb soaring off across the twilight sky.

Now it was Daniel's turn to move. He pointed at the ground and thick ropes burst from the earth, coiling around Sharpe, binding him tight. "How are you here?"

Sharpe looked down at the bindings, then his icy blue eyes stared into Daniel's. He winked, and the ropes around him turned to ash and scattered on the breeze. "You thought you were so clever, didn't you?" He walked slowly forwards. "You thought you had trapped me forever. Thought I was gone. But no, Daniel, I wasn't gone. My soul survived. You'll never understand the places I've been, the power I've seen. I've been to the very heart of the Nowhere Emporium. It is a beautiful sight."

Daniel stepped forward, tried this time to imprison Sharpe in an iron cage, but his old adversary walked through the bars as if he were a ghost.

"You don't understand, do you, Daniel? When you and Ellie Silver banished me, I became part of the

Emporium. I began to grow in strength, and I fed and fed, biding my time all these years."

He snapped his fingers.

Daniel could not move.

He struggled as Sharpe came closer, every part of him on fire with anger and fear and effort. But he was too tired and weak from years of exposure to Sharpe's invisible poison. So that's what had been happening all this time. It had not been, as Daniel had feared, that he wasn't capable of running the shop. Sharpe had been weakening him, waiting to strike. He was standing right in front of Daniel now, huge and menacing. He smelled of decay, and the edges of him were wavering into inky wisps.

"Don't fight it, my boy," Sharpe said, his voice soft. He wiped the sweat from Daniel's brow. "There's no point. You're much too weak. And I? I am only just finding the beginnings of my strength." He took the book from Daniel's hand, and Daniel's eyes filled with tears as he helplessly watched Sharpe open it and flip through the pages.

"Oh, don't worry, Daniel. I'm not going to steal the book. There's no point. I'm part of the Emporium now, part of the book itself. I can never leave. I don't care about the outside world any more. I'm only interested in making this place my kingdom."

He held up the *Book of Wonders*, closed his blue eyes, and the world began to shake. Then, with a flash as bright as an exploding sun, the Carnival of Wonders was gone. In its place was a huge, treasure-filled throne room, with galleried floors stretching up and up forever, all lined with the doors to Daniel's Wonders.

"This is my world now," Sharpe whispered in Daniel's ear. "Look." He snapped his fingers again, and the throne room and all its galleries were suddenly crammed with the Emporium staff and performers, an uncountable number. They seemed stunned to be in these new surroundings, and many yelled out and screamed at the sight of Sharpe.

"My subjects," boomed Sharpe, his voice reverberating around the great throne room and beyond. "Bow before your new king." Another snap of the fingers, and his audience were bowing. Almost all of them; it seemed that there were still a few, dotted here and there, who had not succumbed to Sharpe's magic.

Sweating, pushing against Sharpe's curse with everything he had, Daniel let out a guttural roar, and with a final effort he found he could move again. He broke into a sprint for the red curtain, knowing that if he could get through, Sharpe would not – could not – follow. If he could only get to the front of the shop, he could come up with a plan, maybe go and get help…

When he reached for the curtain, it felt if he had crashed into a solid wall. He bounced off, the wind knocked out of him, and crumpled to the coin-covered floor, where he writhed in agony.

Sharpe helped him up. "I told you: this is my world now. I can only exist behind the curtain, so I need you here too, Daniel. You won't ever be leaving again. The Emporium runs on your imagination, after all. You will stay here with us, powering the Fountain until there is no more magic left in you. Then I will find someone else."

"I'll find a way," choked Daniel, gasping for air.

"No, you won't."

Daniel closed his eyes, and within a second there was a nothing but a blazing fire where he had stood.

"Daniel? Daniel!" Sharpe waved away the smoke. From the flames burst a huge white eagle. "No!" Sharpe dashed forward, but Daniel had already soared high up through the many galleries. "Find him! Bring him to me!" Sharpe cried. "I have trapped him in the Emporium, so leave no stone unturned." He snapped his fingers yet again, and the many Emporium staff and performers transformed into featureless, inky creatures, ready to do his bidding. Nightmares.

As the eagle, Daniel soared up and up and up. His feathers were white as snow, his breast red as blood and the tip of his wings shining gold. He saw his staff become terrible, snarling monsters, and he saw that a few among them had not changed, that they had snuck away to surrounding Wonders as the mass of inky maws stared up at him and howled and moaned.

Daniel was free, and he still had friends in the Emporium. There was hope.

CHAPTER 25

OVER THE EDGE OF THE WORLD

The Nowhere Emporium, Present Day

"*Mes amis*! Wake up! It is time!"

Mirren's eyes cracked open just as Jean Reynard nudged her hammock, causing it to swing wildly.

"What's going on? What's wrong?"

"Nothing is wrong," said Reynard, his eyes twinkling. "It is right! Come and see. We are about to go over the edge!"

Mirren shared bewildered looks with Luke and Robyn, but there was no time for any more questions. Reynard was leading them back to the deck. Here they joined him at the ship's wheel, and he pointed ahead, where the horizon was filled with water vapour, and the light of the moon caught the droplets and split into a hundred moonbows beneath the stars.

"What is that?" asked Luke.

"It is the edge of the world!" cried Reynard, his voice bursting with excitement.

"Wait," said Robyn. "We're not… going over that?"

"*Oui!*" Reynard exclaimed, and his crew let out a great cheer.

"When you say edge…" Mirren said. "There isn't actually an edge, right? The world isn't flat?!" She stopped and considered what she was saying and remembered where she was. "This world *is* flat?"

Jean Reynard let out a bellowing laugh and steadied the wheel, guiding the *Crescent Queen* ever closer to the thundering sound of rushing water and the clouds of vapour.

"But if there's an edge, we'll fall off!" yelled Robyn.

"Why are we even going this way?" Luke held up the compass. "It's telling us to go in the opposite direction. Look!"

Reynard waved his words away like bothersome insects. "You shall see soon enough. Here we go, *mes amis! Allons-y!*"

The ship trembled as the water grew rough, the waves rising, peaked with white foam. The *Crescent Queen* picked up pace as the current took her and threw her forward, and Mirren and her friends yelled out in disbelief and fear as the edge of the world came into view.

It was like they were heading for the biggest waterfall ever, a waterfall that spanned the width of an entire sea. Great torrents of water were crashing over the edge and the vapour in the air was falling back as rain.

Mirren, Luke and Robyn huddled together, clinging on to the ship, hoping that Reynard would change his mind, would come to his senses and spin the wheel and drag the ship away from this terrible fate.

Jean Reynard, though, only smiled, and laughed, and screamed, "HERE WE GO!"

The ship lurched forwards. Mirren could not look away as the edge came nearer, and nearer, and then, with a final, triumphant bellow from Reynard, they fell off the edge of the world.

Only, they did not fall.

The ship tilted headlong, and the world – the entire world – seemed to shift around them. It was impossible. They had gone over the edge, there was no doubt about it. But instead of falling, they had landed on another sea. It was as if the world was a Rubix cube, and they'd been turned from the top surface to one of the sides, then spun back upright.

"Haha!" shouted Jean Reynard. "Was that not exhilarating, *mes amis*? Was it not *magnifique*?"

Mirren found no words.

Robyn, who was never speechless, simply yelled, "You're a madman!"

Luke began to say something but turned green and dashed away to be sick over the side of the ship.

CHAPTER 26

LAST THROW OF THE DICE

The Nowhere Emporium, the Night Daniel Called Mirren

As Mirren slept soundly in her bed, unaware yet that her mum was missing, Daniel Holmes crouched in a forgotten Wonder deep in the Nowhere Emporium, warming himself by a fire. His clothes were ragged, his hair a matted mess, his face gaunt.

It was becoming more and more difficult to find places to hide from Sharpe, to rest, to recharge. Tonight, he found himself in what had once been a Wonder in which customers could fly old Spitfire aeroplanes. He was huddled in the shadow of a Spitfire wreck beneath the stars, sitting in a field of rippling corn.

He stared into the fire, waved his hand over it, and in the flames appeared a vision of the Fountain – or what used to be the Fountain. Now a huge tower of black stone stood over the engine of the Emporium, and atop that tower, Sharpe had her locked away.

Susan Feather.

Until Sharpe brought Susan back, Daniel and his rebellion, the League of the Book, had claimed a number of victories, taking back small pockets of the Emporium. But when Susan arrived, everything had changed. Her power was immense, and Sharpe was somehow controlling her, using her magical strength to feed the Emporium and himself. His power had grown a hundredfold in the following years, and all the while Daniel's had faded. The League of the Book was scattered, reduced to hiding in any safe corner they could find. Daniel's time was almost up.

Almost. But not yet.

Tonight, he would set what might be his last plan in motion. The last throw of the dice. He could not defeat Sharpe single-handedly. But with help…

The objects were in place. It had taken a long time to prepare. Now it was time.

He gathered the last of his strength, waved his hand over the fire again, and in the flames appeared the visions of three sleeping children.

Mirren Feather.

Lukasz Zajac.

Robyn Prince.

He watched them, trying to decide if it was fair to ask this of them, to put such responsibility on their shoulders. They were only children, after all.

No. Not *only* children. Children were powerful in their own ways. They saw things that adults could not. They believed. Had Daniel himself not been just a child when he had defeated Sharpe for the first time? Yes. This was how it had to be.

He reached into his pocket, brought out three feathers: one pure white, one red, one gold. He tossed them up in the air, and they floated into the fire and vanished with a flash. Then Daniel leaned towards the flames, raised his hand, and far off, in Mirren Feather's bedroom, he heard her mobile phone ringing.

"Here we go…"

When it was done, and Mirren and her friends were on their way, Daniel sat back, breathless from the effort, and waited for Sharpe to find him.

It did not take long.

"Hello, Daniel." Sharpe stood over the small fire, the edges of him casting off wisps of inky smoke. "How nice it is to see you at last."

Daniel smiled up at him. "I wish I could say the same."

"Come now. Don't be like that. We all knew how this was going to end. You could not last forever. I had to find someone else to power the Emporium – power *my* world – after you'd gone. Susan Feather is the perfect fit. She is so strong, Daniel. I assume you can feel it?"

"Her power? Yeah, I can feel it. It reminds me of—"

"Lucien Silver?" Sharpe sneered. "I thought that too. But I think Ms Feather has the potential to be even stronger than the great Mr Silver. And unlike him, she doesn't have anyone left to help set her free."

"Oh, I wouldn't be too sure of that," said Daniel.

Sharpe leaned over him. "What are you talking about?" Then he smiled disbelievingly. "Surely you don't mean her daughter? What could a normal child do against me?"

"I think you'll find out soon enough."

A glimmer of worry flashed in Sharpe's crystal-blue eyes, but it was gone in a blink. "Pah. Nonsense. I can't be stopped now."

"And what will you do with me?"

Sharpe smiled. "I'm going to let you linger on. I'm going to make sure you watch as the last of your friends – Caleb, Anja, Ted and the rest – become Nightmares just like all the others. And then, when your heart is broken, I might let you die." He snapped his fingers. "Bring him."

Shaking, weak, Daniel was helpless when a group of Nightmares detached from the shadows among the surrounding field of corn and gathered around him. As they lifted him, the rotting stench of them was choking. They carried him away into the glittering hallways of Sharpe's Emporium palace, and he drifted in and out of consciousness, barely aware of his surroundings, clinging onto hope, knowing the fate of the Nowhere Emporium now rested in the hands of three children.

CHAPTER 27

CALEB

The Nowhere Emporium, Present Day

The *Crescent Queen* sailed on, under a blanket of stars and moonlight, until she pierced a wall of fog so thick that it was difficult to see a few feet in any direction.

"We are close," said Reynard. "Beyond the fog this Wonder ends, and we'll reach the last defence of the League of the Book – one of those few bubbles of safety that remains."

"The League?" Mirren said. "We're going to meet the rest of them?"

"Indeed. And one person in particular." He pointed ahead. "Ah. We arrive."

The thick fog dispersed in moments, uncovering

a small rocky island on which a harbour had been built, and beyond that a village of stone houses. The harbour was loaded with tall ships; Mirren counted nine – though none was as impressive as the *Queen*.

When the *Queen* was moored, Reynard barked at his crew to ready the ship for another journey, and as they set to work, he led Mirren, Luke, Robyn and Anja along the harbour to the tight streets of the village and a house at the top of a bare stony hill overlooking the rest.

Reynard knocked on the door.

Inside the dwelling, a glow of honey-coloured light flickered to life, and then heavy footsteps came towards the door. When it swung open with a creak, Mirren gazed up in amazement at the size of the man who had answered. His barrel chest was bare, save for a black vest, and his tree-trunk legs almost burst from black tights of the sort an acrobat or wrestler might wear. His head was huge and bald, perched on top of a neck as thick as an average person's waist. He filled the entire doorway, every inch of it, and when he looked down at Mirren, his gaze was so fierce that she wanted at first to run away. Then his eyes turned to Anja and his face became childlike.

"Anja," he gasped, his lip quivering. "Is it true? Is it really you?" He rushed forward and hugged her, crying like a massive baby. "Oh, my oldest friend. I thought I'd never see you again."

"It is so good to see you too, Caleb," said Anja, an amused smile on her face. "But we must save the reunion for later. There is work to be done."

Caleb, the big man, broke away from her. "How so?"

With the help of Mirren and her friends, Anja and Jean Reynard quickly told Caleb all about the events of the night, from beginning to end. His eyes grew wide, and he gasped in shock and wonder as they spoke. When they had finished, he simply stood and gazed at Mirren, Lukasz and Robyn with great admiration.

"Good heavens, do you know what this means? It means Daniel is still fighting. It means there is hope. It means that the moment we have been waiting for is finally here! Please, come in." He stood aside as they entered the house, which was small and bare. Showing them to the kitchen, he indicated a rustic table. "Please, sit." Caleb sat at the head, the wooden chair groaning under his weight. He looked around at them again, as if he was struggling to believe what he was seeing. "Susie Feather's daughter, eh? Your mother was quite the flavour of the month with Daniel way back, you know. She would have been a great apprentice, I think."

Mirren brought out the snow globe containing her mum's secret and placed it on the table. Caleb stared into it, at the low sun and the two figures standing upon the frozen pond.

"The Fountain!"

"Do you know where this is?" Mirren asked.

He shook his huge head. "Nobody does. Sharpe has hidden it away."

"We think it's where he's keeping my mum."

"We also think," added Anja, "that the Fountain is where Sharpe's power – what is left of his soul – is hiding."

Caleb gave a nod. "Daniel has not been in touch for a very long time. Even when he was on the run, he always made contact every now and then. I fear, as I am sure you do, Jean and Anja, that Sharpe has finally captured him. If Sharpe is keeping Susan in the Fountain, then it makes sense that Daniel is there too."

"We have to help them." Anja had come around and placed a hand on Mirren's shoulder.

"Yes," said Caleb, "we do. And by the sounds of it, Daniel has given you three the tools to succeed. The key…" He nodded to Robyn. "It could take you there."

She brought the key out. It was almost unrecognisable, half rusted away. "We don't know if it still works. Sharpe's poison is ruining it. And even if it does work, how do I open a door to the right place?"

"You must use everything you have. You must tell it with your mind and your soul and your heart." Caleb pressed the tips of his huge fingers together.

"We have been waiting a very long time for the right moment to make our move. That time is now. We must get you to the Fountain. There, the fate of the Nowhere Emporium will be decided."

"They'll be waiting," said Jean Reynard. "Sharpe will send whatever he can to stop them."

Caleb stood up. "We have an army of our own to occupy Sharpe's Nightmares. We'll be the distraction."

CHAPTER 28

THE LEAGUE'S LAST STAND

The Nowhere Emporium, Present Day

Ten ships left the harbour, led by Jean Reynard and the *Crescent Queen*. On each ship stood a hundred characters brought to life by the pages of a magic book, ready to fight – to face oblivion – to save their home.

Mirren, Luke and Robyn stood at the wheel with Reynard, Caleb and Anja, letting the glowing dial of the compass guide them through the fog and over the edge of the world again to another ocean; this one a vast expanse of stormy, high-peaked waves that carried the ships up and tossed them around like toys.

The sky was laden with angry thunderclouds, and when the first forks of lightning struck at the horizon, they lit the armada that Vindictus Sharpe had sent to meet the League. A hundred ships, maybe more, came cutting through the waves. They started out as nothing more than black dots, but after a while Mirren could see sails, and armies of those terrible Nightmares on the decks and clinging to the masts, screaming and grunting and snarling.

Mirren felt a hand take hers and realised that it was Robyn's. She looked at her and smiled, and Robyn smiled back. Then Luke put a hand on her shoulder, and they stood, three friends who would work together to face whatever was to come.

"You ready?" Mirren asked.

"No," said Luke.

"Nope," said Robyn.

"Good. Me neither."

"You must go now, *mes amis*," instructed Reynard. "They are almost upon us."

Robyn took the crumbling key from her pocket as the ship rose and fell with the waves. "I hope it works one last time."

"Remember," said Caleb, "you must concentrate on the place that you wish to go. Visualise the Fountain in your mind. Have confidence that you will get it right, that the magic Daniel has given you – the feathers, the compass – will work together and find the Fountain where we could not."

"You can do it," said Anja. "We all believe in you."

Robyn set her jaw and gave a nod. She took the key, held it out, slipped it into an invisible lock. "The Fountain," she repeated to herself over and over. "The Fountain."

"It's working!" Luke pointed to the blazing outline that was appearing in the air before them.

"It is!" said Mirren. "Go, Robyn!"

Robyn smiled, her eyes widening as the door began to appear…

BOOM!

A massive explosion nearby sent pieces of the ship flying everywhere. The *Crescent Queen* lurched sideways. Mirren hit the floor, looked up to see Robyn sliding down the slippery deck and off the missing side of the ship into the stormy water.

"Robyn!" Mirren scrambled to her feet, stumbled to what was left of the gunwale, stared over. The first arrows began to rain down from the approaching fleet.

Shoof!

Shoof-Shoof-Shoof!

The Nightmare boats were close now, their crews beginning to swing across on ropes, even leaping from ship to ship to engage in combat with the waiting League of the Book.

"There!" Mirren spotted Robyn in the water, struggling as she was carried high then low on great waves. Without thinking, she jumped.

She hit the icy water, plunged deep below the surface, and as she swam back up she could hear the muffled booms and bangs of the fighting above, and see flashes of cannon fire.

Her head found clean air, and she took a deep breath, saw Robyn struggling to stay afloat a distance away. Mirren swam, her arm cutting through the harsh water, her strong legs propelling her.

"Robyn! I'm coming!"

"Mirren! Mirren, help! I can't—" Robyn, who was not as strong a swimmer as Mirren, disappeared under the waves for a long moment, and came back up spitting out water.

"Hang on!" Mirren swam faster, pulled up and down with the waves. Finally, Robyn reached out and clung onto her, grabbing at her clothes until she got her breath back.

"I managed…" She spat out a mouthful of water. "I managed to hold onto the key. I've still got it!"

A deep voice called out, "Here, take Luke's hand." Caleb was rowing a small boat, his great arms carrying it up and over mountainous waves. Luke leaned over the edge, reaching out for Mirren and Robyn. All the while the air was rent with the boom of cannon fire and the clang of duelling blades. There were screams and grunts, Nightmares and League fighters alike tumbling to the water, exploding in clouds of ink as they met their end.

"Almost there!" Luke yelled.

Just as the rowing boat reached them, it rocked as a Nightmare, made of shadow and ink, landed aboard. It leapt upon Caleb, and as they struggled Luke tumbled into the water. He swam through the towering waves to reach his friends, grabbing a piece of wreckage as he went, tossing it to Robyn so that she could use it as a float. "We have to go! Now!"

There were ships on fire, acrid smoke billowing around them, the burning glow of the flames reflecting on the stormy water. A great explosion nearby made pieces of burning ships rain down.

"Use the key!"

"Will it work in the water?"

"Try it! Hurry!"

Clinging to her makeshift float, Robyn reached out, dipped the key into the water and turned it. Amazingly, a burning outline appeared on the surface beside her, and then, in a flash, there was the door, floating in the water. Luke was already swimming for it, almost there, and Mirren thanked her stars as she pulled herself through the waves that her mum had taken her swimming so often.

Finally, after what felt like an eternity, they reached Robyn and the door; Luke pulled it open just as another wave carried them ten metres into the air. As it began to fall, and their stomachs lurched, the three friends tumbled through the opening and down into the unknown.

CHAPTER 29
THE TOWER

The Nowhere Emporium, Present Day

Thud.

They landed on hard, frosty ground. Mirren rolled over, just in time to see Luke shambling towards an open door standing on the ice. Through the doorway came the thundering sounds of the world they'd just left, cannon fire and lightning and crashing waves, until Luke slammed the door shut and all fell to silence.

"You OK, Mirren?" Robyn offered a hand.

Mirren took it, allowed Robyn to help her up. She recognised her surroundings at once. Excited, she pulled the snow globe from her pocket and held it out.

They were standing in the very scene depicted in the globe, on a frozen pond under a crystal-blue sky. Only, instead of a pretty stone fountain standing in the middle of the pond, there was a great ragged tower of black stone.

"You did it, Robyn!" said Luke. "You opened a door to the right place."

"You were amazing!" said Mirren.

Slowly, they approached the tower, staring up at the vast scale of it. At the highest point, a sharp stone finger reached out as if to pierce the perfect sky.

They were sodden and freezing, shivering in the cold, but that didn't matter now. All that mattered was getting to the top of the tower. Mirren knew this somehow, and the compass confirmed it when it led them to a tall arched doorway at the base of the structure. As they approached, the doorway swung open, revealing a dark staircase that spiralled up to a dizzying height.

"I guess there's only one thing to do, eh?" said Mirren, and she put her foot on the first step.

"'Wait," said Robyn. "What's that? You hear it? I think someone is here."

She was right. A faint voice was whispering in the quiet.

"You're here," it said, again and again.

They followed it up the steps, arriving soon at a heavy metal door. In the door was a small barred window, and when they looked through they saw a teenage boy crumpled in a dark corner, illuminated by the light from a tiny window.

"You're here. I knew you'd come."

Mirren felt such pity for this wretched creature that tears welled in her eyes. Then a thought struck her, and her eyes widened. "Daniel? Daniel Holmes… is that you?"

He struggled to sit up, slumped against the damp stone wall, turned his head to face them. He was filthy, and his hair was long and matted. His clothes were torn, and he was painfully thin. Yet his eyes were bright, and he smiled when he saw them. "I knew… I knew you could do it."

Mirren grabbed the door, tried to push and pull it open. "Help me, Robyn, Luke. Help me get him out."

"It's no use," said Daniel, his voice gravelly and dry. "Only Sharpe can open it. Your job isn't done yet. You have to get to the top of the tower."

"But—"

"You must. You'll find your mum there. Together you can beat him. Go. Go now, please…"

"OK," said Mirren. "But we'll come back for you. I promise."

It was difficult to leave him like that, but they forced themselves to move on.

They climbed.

And climbed.

And climbed, until their lungs were screaming, their legs on fire, their muscles ready to melt away. Still they pushed on. Whenever one became tired or stopped, the others would encourage their friend to keep going.

Each of them had their moments. Even Mirren, who would have died there and then to save her mum, thought on several occasions that she could not continue. Each time her friends were there, and she carried on.

After what may have been hours, or might have been days, they reached the summit of the dark staircase. There they found another doorway, and Mirren knew in her heart that this would be the last.

She swallowed, squeezed another breath into her exhausted body. She was afraid. If Mum really was on the other side of this door, if she really had been trapped here for many years, what was Mirren going to find?

"We're here, Mir." Luke's voice brought her back, pushed the fear away a little.

"Yeah," said Robyn. "We'll be with you every step."

Their words were a warm blanket around her, casting off the icy chill that had set in around her heart.

Knowing that her friends were by her side, Mirren Feather reached out, grabbed the handle, and opened the door.

CHAPTER 30

AT THE TOP OF THE TOWER

The Nowhere Emporium, Present Day

Mirren had been expecting darkness. Her head had been filled with visions of a tiny cell, like the one in which Daniel Holmes was trapped, her mother huddled in the corner, shivering and weeping.

When the door opened, they were instead greeted by dazzling light. The room was huge and circular, and made not of black stone, but of shining, pure crystal. Every wall, every object in the place, seemed to glow in the light of the sun. The room was filled with furniture – a four-poster bed, a long couch and a dressing table – all were made of the same gleaming crystal. There was a bookcase made of crystal, stacked with crystal books, and a strange, blue-flamed fire burned in a crystal mantel.

Standing by the window with her back to Mirren and her friends, gazing out at the winter landscape, was a woman in a long white gown that sparkled and shimmered as if it was coated in frost.

For the longest time Mirren could not move. She only stood in the doorway and stared at the woman by the window, at the auburn hair tumbling over her shoulders. At last, she stepped forward slowly, her eyes fixed on the figure. "Mum?"

The woman's head moved ever so slightly. Then she turned around.

Mirren's eyes lit up. It was Mum. She had been so terrified that after years and years in this place Mum would be an old lady. But, if anything, she looked younger and more beautiful than Mirren could ever remember. Her skin was flawless and smooth, the worry lines gone from around her dazzling green eyes. Her auburn hair was arranged in shining ribbons. Her lips were ruby red. It seemed, as Mirren looked at her, that Mum was glowing, that the very air around her was alive.

Mirren hurried forward and threw herself at her mum, wrapping her arms around her, squeezing, telling herself she'd never let go.

But her mum did not hug back.

And she was cold.

Mirren's joy turned quickly to fear. She broke away, backed off a step, then two, and three. She looked into those emerald eyes and saw that there was no warmth or love in them. "Mum? Mum, it's me."

Mum looked her up and down. "Oh? And who exactly are you?"

The words were sharp; Mirren felt them cut into her heart. She glanced back at her friends, still in the doorway, and they nodded encouragement. "Mum," she said again. "Mum, it's me. Mirren. Your daughter."

Susan Feather let out a musical laugh, light and carefree. "Don't be silly, child. I don't have a daughter. I don't have anyone, in fact." She went back to the window, looked out at the forever blue sky. "It's just me in my tower, and that's how I like it."

"But Mum!" That ball of dread was back in Mirren's stomach, heavy as lead, pulling her down towards despair.

Mum turned her attention back to Mirren. "You are mistaken, girl. If your mother is in the Emporium, you won't find her here."

The tears came now, spilling over, hot and stinging in the freezing cold of the tower. "Mum. Please…" And then Luke and Robyn were at her side, standing shoulder to shoulder with her. "What do I do?" she asked them helplessly. "What am I supposed to do?"

There were tears in Luke's eyes too, and in Robyn's.

"I don't know," admitted Luke.

"But we're with you," said Robyn.

"HOW TOUCHING."

The voice was so loud and deep that it shook the tower, and Mirren felt it in her bones.

Robyn screamed, pointed a trembling finger towards the arched window on the opposite side of the room.

Mirren took a sharp breath. She was instantly paralysed by fear. There, filling almost the entire window, was the icy blue eye of a giant. The three friends could do nothing but stand frozen, staring back at that enormous eye as it flicked between them.

"Oh," said Mirren's mum. "Don't worry about him. He turns up sometimes to check on his friend." She pointed downwards, and Mirren realised that she meant Daniel Holmes, imprisoned in his cell.

"He's not Daniel's friend. And he's done something to you, Mum! Remember, please!"

A flash of light. The eye was gone from the window, and a tall, broad-shouldered man stood in the chamber with them. He had neatly cropped silver hair and a square jaw, and his eyes were the same icy blue as the giant's. He stared down at Mirren and her friends, and the ferocity of his gaze made them shrink back a little.

"You," he said, "have been a pain in my backside." He flicked a glance towards Mirren's mum. "Take their feathers."

Susan gave him a blank look. "What?"

"They have feathers. Take them."

Susan gave an impatient sigh. "If I do that, will you all leave me alone?"

"Yes," said the man.

"Mum. No!"

But it was too late; Susan held out an open hand, and the feathers – one white, one red, one gold, the colour of the great bird Daniel had once become to soar over the Emporium – flew out of the children's pockets and into her waiting palm.

From far below, a moan echoed through the tower.

"Shut up!" screamed the man with the silver hair. He pointed at the floor, and Daniel's moan turned into a scream of agony.

"Stop!' yelled Robyn. "Stop hurting him!"

Surprisingly, he did. He lowered his hand and stared across the room at the three children.

"You said you'd all leave me alone," said Susan Feather.

"Yes," said the man. "We will. But before I go, I'd like to give you a gift."

Susan's eyebrows arched. "A gift?"

"Yes. This place is very nice, but maybe you would like a few ornaments to brighten it up?" He turned towards Mirren and her friends again and pointed, and at once Mirren could feel that something was terribly wrong.

Her feet had begun to grow very cold, and when she looked down, she saw that they had turned to ice, and that the ice was creeping up her ankles, and her shins, and her knees.

"Mir?" The same was happening to Luke and Robyn. The ice had already reached their thighs. They tried to move but found that they could not.

"No!" cried Robyn. "No!"

Mirren watched in terror as the ice reached her friend's neck, and crawled up her face, and closed over her head. And the same happened to Luke. There were tears in his eyes as he turned his head towards her. "Mir," he said. "Mirren…" But he could not finish, for the curse had overcome him too, turned him into an ice sculpture.

The ice was moving slower up Mirren's body; it had reached her thighs. She shot a desperate look towards the man with the silver hair, who smiled like a wolf.

As more and more of her froze, Mirren's mind searched for a way out, for anything that might help. And then, a voice in her head said, "Mirren."

She knew at once that it was coming from the cell far below.

"Use your memories, Mirren. Use the good times."

Most of Mirren's right side was now ice; she felt it spreading, felt what was left of herself drifting away, shrinking smaller and smaller as it fell towards the dark.

The ice crept up her jaw, her face, her nose, until only her eyes remained. She took one last look at her mum, drinking the image of her in, and she knew she'd soon be gone.

Everything would be gone.

With a desperate, agonising effort, she tried to think of a happy time…

Mum's smile of pride when Mirren had first managed to swim a length of the local pool.

The ice stopped creeping. Mirren felt a spark of warmth in her chest, like a miraculous candle pushing back a little of the dark.

Our holidays in St Andrews.

The flame in her chest burned brighter. The ice began to crack, to recede.

"No." Beads of sweat were forming on Sharpe's forehead. "No!"

Mirren clung on to the happy memories. One by one they came.

Mirren's first swimming trophy, Mum cheering her on from the crowd…

Mum's birthday last year, when Mirren had made her breakfast in bed and she had eaten the slightly burnt toast as if it had been the most delicious meal in the world…

The notes they left each other on the fridge chalkboard…

Bedtime stories and songs when Mirren was little…

Falling asleep together under a blanket on the couch on rainy weekends…

Each memory burned brighter than the last, melted Mirren's icy prison, cracked it, until at last it shattered, exploding outwards, falling to the crystal floor in a thousand frozen fragments.

"Impossible," cried Sharpe. "I will not allow it!" He rushed forward, but before he could get to her, Mirren took the snow globe and tossed it across the room towards her mum, watching with hope as it arced through the air.

CHAPTER 31
BROKEN GLASS

The Nowhere Emporium, Present Day

Susan Feather had watched with a sense of great curiosity as the children in her chamber turned to ice. First the girl in pink, then the boy. And finally, the girl with one arm, who was obviously the leader. But then the leader-girl had done something strange and unexpected. She had fought back. Somehow, she had repelled Sharpe's curse, shattered the ice, and thrown something towards Susan.

The snow globe stopped, hung frozen in the air.

Across the room, Vindictus Sharpe stood with a hand reaching out. He beckoned with a finger, and the globe moved towards him.

Then it stopped.

Sharpe stared at his fingers, confused, and tried with the other hand.

The same thing happened.

He turned his hands over, inspecting them, and tried once more to bring the globe towards him. Beads of sweat gathered on his brow as he used all his considerable strength. Still it was no good. He straightened up, panting, sweating, as if he'd been in a fight. When he felt Susan Feather's eyes upon him and spun around to face her, he knew at once what had occurred. She stood by the window, her arm outstretched, the fingers of her half-closed hand pointed towards the crystal sphere. She had stopped him. But how? She could not possibly remember who she was…

"Take it!" the leader-girl was shouting. "Take the snow globe. It's yours!"

"She's lying," said Sharpe. "It'll hurt you!"

Susan took a step closer to the girl. There was something familiar about her, and the familiarity brought a feeling that there was an undiscovered river of memories waiting beneath the surface of her mind if she could only break through.

"I'm telling you!" said Sharpe, and there was fear and anger in his voice. "Leave it alone!"

He stormed towards her, but she raised a casual hand and sent him flying across the room, dropping to the floor beneath the window with a loud thud.

With no more distractions, Susan beckoned the snow globe towards her. When it landed in her waiting palms, she was surprised to find that her hands trembled. Warmth radiated from the globe, spread up her arms and through her body. She could not understand why there were tears in her eyes. She cast a glance towards Sharpe.

"Please," he implored, reaching out. "Don't."

But she had already let the snow globe fall. She knew that it had to be opened, and that she was the only one who could do it. The crystal globe tumbled from her fingers and shattered on the ground, and Susan Feather's memories filled the room.

CHAPTER 32

AWAKE

The Nowhere Emporium, Present Day

Susan remembered everything.

"Mirren?" She blinked, her wide green eyes drinking in the sight of her beautiful daughter. "What are you doing here? Are you OK?" She dashed forward, the memories blossoming in her head like spring flowers. "Oh, my girl. My sunshine! What did he try to do to you?"

"Mum! You're back!" Mirren flew forward, grabbed her mum into the tightest of hugs. Susan smelled her daughter's hair, kissed her head, her nose, her cheeks, and all the while Luke and Robyn were returning, flesh and blood once more.

"You remember me!" said Mirren.

"Of course I remember you," said Mum. "You're my everything!"

"No!" spat a forgotten voice from across the room. "I will not stand for it. Not after everything I've been through. Not after all the time I waited!"

Vindictus Sharpe was back on his feet. His face was filled with hate and madness, his icy blue eyes wide and wild. Quite out of his mind, he shambled forward, scratching and clawing towards Mirren, but Susan stepped between them and threw up her hands and screamed, sending a shockwave at Sharpe that blew him through the wall and down, down, down towards the icy pond. They ran to the window in time to see Sharpe crashing through the ice, leaving a cloud of inky smoke in the air.

Mirren hugged Luke and Robyn tight, but the celebrations were cut short when the tower began to rumble and shake and fall apart, huge crystal chunks and shards crashing down all around.

"We need to get out of here!" yelled Susan. "Hurry. With me!"

She led them to the top of the spiral staircase, clicked her fingers, and the stairs vanished and became an icy slide. Down they went, whooshing around and around at tremendous speed, while the walls were trembling and crumbling. All around, the world seemed to be splitting apart; the sound was deafening, the air rent with rumbles and thunderous bangs.

"Daniel!" said Mirren when they came to the end of the slide at last. "What about Daniel?"

The slide became stairs again, and they dashed up to the heavy cell door. Susan threw out a hand and the door turned to dust. Inside the cell, Daniel was on one knee, trying to get up. Mirren and her mum rushed in, helped him stand, held him as they hurried down the remaining stairs and out through the door to the frozen pond, scrambling across as fast as they could to the shelter of the trees. There they watched the tower fall, crashing to the ice, sending a gigantic plume of frosty cloud rolling out across the landscape. As the cloud tore towards them, Mirren and her friends dove for cover behind the great oak trees, sheltering their faces as the ice cloud roared all around.

The sound reached a thunderous crescendo, and Mirren imagine that the entire Wonder was ripping apart, that the ground might crack open and swallow her friends. Then, in a heartbeat, the rumble died away, and all was quiet and calm. They crept slowly out from the trees and saw, to their amazement, that there was no trace the tower had ever been there: no rubble, no hint of crystal shard. The ice of the pond looked sleek and untouched, and in the centre stood a stone fountain running with fine silvery liquid.

"Is he OK?" Luke crouched over Daniel. He lay still on the frosted ground, a boy in his mid-teens, with longish red hair and a face that might one day become handsome. He looked peaceful.

Susan took his hand, squeezing it. She did not speak. Nobody spoke until Daniel Holmes's eyes opened a fraction, and he blinked a few times, clearing the cobwebs from his mind. When his eyes focused properly, he stared up at Susan, and a wide smile broke over his face. "Susan?" He sat up.

"Careful," she said. "Take it easy."

"I'll live," he said, and struggled to his feet. There followed a very long moment when Daniel and Susan simply stood staring at each other. Mirren thought they might be about to fight, but instead they smiled and hugged each other.

"There was a time I thought I'd never see you again," he told her.

"Me too," she said.

Susan looked at her mum; the worry lines were back around her eyes, and her hair was a little messy. She no longer looked like a too-perfect, idealised version of herself, and Mirren was very glad of that.

"I'm sorry, Daniel," said Susan. "This was all my fault. Sharpe would never have come back in the first place if I hadn't—"

"Tried to help?" He finished her sentence. "You were trying to do the right thing, Susan. I was tired.

I was losing control of the Emporium, just as Mr Silver had done before me. I didn't know what was causing it, but now I do: it was Sharpe. He was spreading through the place like poison, weakening me. If I were you, I'd have done the same thing. There's nothing to be sorry about. In fact, if anyone should be apologising it's me."

"Whatever for?" said Susan.

Daniel's eyes brimmed. "For not being strong enough to stop Sharpe. For letting him put you through this. And for putting your daughter in danger." At this he turned to Mirren and her friends, and took Mirren's hand in his. "I was desperate. I had been trying to fight him for the longest time. Then, when he brought your mum back, used her power against me, I couldn't see any other way to stop him. I would never have asked so much of you if there had been another way, you see? I knew you were the only one, Mirren, who could make your mum remember."

Mirren nodded, and Luke and Robyn came to her side. "I understand. I'd have done anything to get Mum back. And I wasn't alone."

Daniel looked around at the three friends. "No. You weren't. At least I got that bit right. Come."

He led them to the fountain, where silvery liquid was flowing freely over the circles of stone.

"It's beautiful," said Robyn, awe in her voice.

"Isn't it?" Daniel reached into the liquid imagination – pure magic – and splashed a little over his face. He seemed to grow a little stronger. Then he stopped, and Mirren clocked that he was now staring past her, his mouth hanging a little open. She turned to see what he was looking at, and saw, to her horror, a huge hand punch through the ice from beneath the surface. Then, gripping the icy crust, another hand appeared, and Vindictus Sharpe heaved himself up from the pond and landed heavily on the frozen ground. He dragged himself to his full height and stared across the ice at them.

"It's over, Sharpe." Daniel stepped forward, between Sharpe and the children.

Inky liquid was dripping from Sharpe's nose and from the corner of his mouth. He spat a glob of it onto the ice. "It will never be over," he said. "Don't you see? Lucien Silver created this place and even he couldn't finish me off. What chance do you have? I'm part of the Emporium now. I will live forever."

Daniel clenched his jaw. "I've been thinking about this moment for a long time, imagining what I'll do to you when I finally get the chance. Do you know what I'm going to do, Sharpe?"

Sharpe took a step forward, clenched his fists and snarled. "What?"

Daniel too stepped forward, his eyes burning into

Sharpe's. When he spoke, his voice was soft. "*I'm going to do nothing.*"

"What?" repeated Sharpe.

Daniel spun to face Susan. "The book!" he yelled. "Use it!"

She looked at him, bewildered for a moment, and then a flare of certainty lit up in her mind, and she knew what he was asking. She held out an open hand, thought of the book.

Sharpe swung his head towards her, his eyes wide. "No!"

But the *Book of Wonders* had already been ripped from his coat, was flying through the air, and it landed in Susan's waiting hand.

Sharpe let out a terrible scream, ran forward.

Susan was calm. She opened the *Book of Wonders* to blank pages and closed her eyes.

To Mirren's astonishment, something appeared on the pages. At first, she thought it was a splotch of ink, but as it grew, she saw that it was not that at all.

It was a hole.

A hole in the book. A hole in the reality of the Emporium.

"Children!" yelled Daniel. "Do you still have your feathers?"

"I've still got them," said Susan. She held out the feathers. "Take them back, quick."

They took them, one white, one red, one gold.

"Touch them together," said Daniel. "Use the magic I locked away within them."

Mirren held out her feather, as did Robyn and Luke. When the feathers touched, there was a bright flash and spark, and Mirren felt the power of the Emporium flowing through her, all of that endless imagination and magic in her veins.

Sharpe tried to skid to a stop, but a howling gale burst from the point in reality where the feathers touched; it sounded like a million people all screaming at once. Mirren and her friends huddled together, redoubled their efforts, pointing the feathers at Sharpe as the magical storm wrapped around him, dragged him ever closer to the book.

Sharpe was twisting and flailing, his feet scraping deep grooves in the ice as he tried to get away. But there was no escape. The book pulled him, and the gale pushed him. His outline became smoky, inky, as the hole sucked him in little by little, until only his head remained, and then that was eaten too, with a final, outraged scream.

Susan Feather slammed the book shut.

CHAPTER 33

GOODBYES

The Nowhere Emporium, Present Day

Silence.

Then cheers. Not from Mirren and her friends, or Daniel, or Susan, but from the many Emporium staff who had felt the tower fall and rushed to the Fountain, able to find it once more. They charged the icy pond from the woods in every direction. They flooded onto the ice, surrounding the heroes, lifting them high and cheering their names.

"My friends!" came a cry among the happy chaos. "You have done it! I knew you would!"

Mirren, Luke and Robyn ran at Ted the metal man, hugging him, shaking his hand.

"You made it!" they cried. "You're OK!"

"It'll take more than a few Nightmares to make a dent in this armour." He winked a glowing glass eye.

Anja was there too, and Caleb, and Jean Reynard, congratulating the children, shaking hands with Susan, hugging Daniel.

"Sharpe's Nightmares are gone," said Caleb. "As soon as they disappeared, we knew that you had prevailed. Today is a great day! The Nowhere Emporium is free once again!"

The celebrations lasted for days, with feasts and dancing and singing. They ate roast beef and Yorkshire puddings, aromatic curry, platters of fresh fruit and vegetables, sumptuous chocolate cake and a hundred flavours of ice cream, every course more wonderful than the last.

When it was time to go, Daniel walked them to the front of the shop. Sharpe's throne room was gone, replaced by the Carnival of Wonders under the twilight sky, and the place was filled with performers and lights and the smells of candied almonds and popcorn.

Then it was through the red curtain, where the shop was waiting, quiet and dusty and dark. The only sounds were the myriad ticking clocks and the gentle spit of the fire.

Daniel took the Emporium to Robyn's street first.

"Won't my mum be worried about me? I've been gone ages!"

"No," said Daniel. "For anyone on the outside, only a few minutes have passed since you came here. She won't even know you've been out of bed." He winked. "If you're quiet, that is."

Robyn nodded. Mirren ran forward and hugged her, and when Luke did the same, Robyn turned a burning shade of red.

"Bye, Robyn. And thanks."

"Bye," she said. She went to the shop door and opened it, but before she left, she paused. Her face was very serious, frightened almost.

"What's wrong?" Mirren asked.

"I'm scared. I'm scared that, as soon as I leave here, the magic will wear off. I'm scared I'll wake up tomorrow and everything'll be just like it was before. I want… I want us to stay friends."

Mirren and Luke looked at each other, and then at Robyn.

"Robyn," said Mirren with a smile. "You're not going to get rid of us that easily."

"We know you now," said Luke. "The *real* you. That's who we want to be friends with. And I reckon if you show that person to the world, lots more people will feel the same."

"Really?" Robyn smiled and dabbed her eyes.

"Right," she said, taking a deep breath. "Well, here goes, I guess. I'll see you guys tomorrow?"

Mirren smiled warmly. "Bet on it."

They watched through the window as Robyn snuck back into a big detached house across the street. Then the Emporium was moving again.

"Next stop!" said Daniel.

Luke went to the door, opened it, and gasped. "We're outside my front door!"

"Yes," said Daniel. "We are."

"But I live on the fourteenth floor!" said Luke in disbelief.

Mirren laughed. "Does anything really surprise you any more?"

He laughed too. "No, I guess not. Some night, eh?"

"We've had quieter ones."

Luke chuckled. "And what about Robyn! You think she's really turned over a new leaf?"

Mirren nodded. "I hope so. She doesn't have it as easy as we thought, you know."

"How d'you mean?"

"I'll let her explain when she's ready," said Mirren.

"Cool. I guess I'd better go, let you get home."

"Yeah."

Mirren watched him go. When he'd opened the door to the flat, she said, "Hey, Luke?"

"Yeah?"

"You're a good friend."

"I know." He gave her a wide, goofy smile. "I'm the best." Then he shut the door behind him.

After that, the Emporium took them back to the High Street. The final stop.

"Are you OK?" Susan asked Daniel. "You look terrible."

"Oh, well thank you very much," he said.

"I didn't mean… I just *meant*…"

"I know, I'm only joking. I'm fine. Just tired." But there was something in his eyes that said it was more than that. "I've thanked you both a hundred times. But here's one more: thank you."

They went to the shop door, and through the glass Mirren saw the old, familiar world. It seemed unthinkable that they'd be going back to everyday life without magic. Without the Emporium.

"Will you both come back tomorrow? Eight o'clock in the evening? There's something I want to give you."

Mirren and Susan exchanged curious glances. "Sure," said Susan. "We'll be here."

Half an hour later, Mirren was back in bed. Mum sat with her, stroking her hair. Mirren's eyelids grew heavy, her every blink lasting just a bit longer.

"Love you, Mum."

"Love you too, sunshine. Hey, Mir?"

"Yeah?"

"I know you're far too old for this now, but would you mind if I sing you to sleep like I did when you were wee? Just this one night?"

Mirren smiled sleepily. "I'd love it."

Mum began to sing, and Mirren fell asleep knowing all was well with the world.

CHAPTER 34
ENDINGS AND BEGINNINGS

The Nowhere Emporium, Elmbank, near Glasgow, Present Day

Mirren and Susan knocked on the door of the Nowhere Emporium at eight o'clock sharp the next night, just as Daniel had requested.

When he answered, it struck Mirren right away how young he looked. The night before, his eyes had been those of someone so much older.

Tonight, his eyes sparkled.

"Come," he said, his movements all jangling and excited. "Come with me!"

They followed him through the front of the shop, through the curtain to the Carnival of Wonders.

They walked and walked, between towering striped tents, until, at last, they came to a clearing where hundreds of performers and staff had gathered, their colourful clothes glowing in the light of the red-gold sky.

As they approached, the crowd parted for them until they reached the centre. Here stood a curious-looking doorway: just a frame and a simple black door that seemed to lead to nowhere. Mirren looked around the surrounding audience, saw Jean Reynard and Caleb, Anja and Ted. She waved at them, and they waved back.

"Daniel," said Susan, "what's this all about?"

Daniel smiled, and brushed his red hair from his eyes. "I asked you to come back tonight so that I could give you something, remember?"

Susan nodded. "Ye-es…" She was using the same voice as when she suspected that Mirren had been up to no good.

Daniel smiled again; he seemed so happy, so… light. He reached into his jacket, then stopped and said, "Close your eyes. Both of you."

"What? Why?"

"Just do it, will you? Don't spoil the moment."

"Fine." Susan and Mirren shared a shrug and closed their eyes.

Mirren heard Daniel fidgeting, then he said, "OK. Open them."

When Mirren opened her eyes, the first thing she saw was Daniel smiling. Then she turned to Mum and saw that she was holding a black book in her hands, looking from it to Daniel and back again.

"I don't get it," Susan said.

"It's yours," said Daniel. "I brought you here because… the thing I wanted to give you… it's the Nowhere Emporium."

There were gasps from the crowd. Susan said nothing. She simply gawped at Daniel.

"Well?" he said. "Say something, will you!"

"Daniel, I… I can't take this. The Emporium is yours!"

He shook his head. "My time is coming to an end."

"But you're still only…"

"What?" he said. "A teenager? I might look young, Susan, but I've lived a hundred lives. I've been all around the world. I've seen many things I want to remember forever, and some things I want to forget. I'm tired, Susan – just like Mr Silver was tired when he handed the Emporium to me. Struggling against Sharpe all these years has taken just about the last of the power I had left."

"But I can't! I don't know how!"

"Nobody knows how!" said Daniel with a laugh. "I certainly didn't." He came forward, tapped the cover of the book. "You have a connection to this place. The Nowhere Emporium has chosen you as much as I have. It's meant to be."

Susan was shaking. "But I… but… what do you think, Mir?"

Mirren's head was spinning, and yet she had one very clear thought. "I think this is the most magical place in all the world," she said. "And I think… I think he's right. You are special. I've always known it."

"But I can't just up and leave," said Susan. "I've got Mirren. She has school, and friends. I won't take her away from any of that."

Daniel held his hands up. "You won't have to, nor would I want you to. You can take this as slowly as you like. Spend years getting to know the place, practising, getting everything how you want it. Then, when you're ready… blast off."

"Blast off," whispered Mirren with a smile.

Mum was smiling too, and biting her lip, and Mirren knew that meant she'd already made up her mind.

"But where will you go?" Susan asked. "Back to Glasgow?"

Daniel shook his head. For the first time that night, Mirren saw a hint of that age creeping back into his eyes. "No. I can't go back out there. I don't belong now. And with all the magic I've spent fighting, I wouldn't last long outside the Emporium. I have another plan." He walked to the doorway, leaned on the doorframe and brought another book out from his jacket, this one much smaller, like an address book. "It's my own *Book of Wonders*. It means I can write Wonders just for me. Whole worlds I can explore. A place I can grow old and live a good life."

"Through there?" said Susan, motioning to the doorway. "But that's great! It means we can visit you!"

Daniel smiled. He came forward again, took her hand. "I'll keep an eye on you. And if you need me, I'll be there."

Susan squeezed his hand. "Are you sure about this?"

He suddenly looked younger than ever. "I've never been surer of anything."

Susan pulled him into a hug. "Thank you, Daniel Holmes. Thank you for everything."

He stepped back, and there was no sadness in his face now. Looking all around the crowd, he said, "My friends, it has been an honour. I might be stepping down, but the Nowhere Emporium will go on. It will go on forever, I think, as long as it stays in the right hands. I have already spoken to many of you in person, told you of my plan to leave." At this he paused, and met the eyes of Caleb, Anja, Ted and the others. He gave a nod and a smile, and they returned the gesture. "But here and now, I want to say thank you to all of you for giving a poor wee orphan from Glasgow the most wonderful life. Now I continue my journey. I want you to know that I'll never forget you."

"Thank you, Daniel," came shouts from the crowd.

"We love you, Mr Holmes!"

"Long live Daniel Holmes!"

"Three cheers for Daniel!"

Daniel looked at Mirren, and with a wink said, "Look after your mum, kid."

As he walked towards the door, the place grew very quiet. The only sound came from way up in the sky, where two silver magpies circled high overhead, calling out.

Daniel opened the door to a beautiful beach and a sapphire sea. Warm air drifted through the doorway, carrying the scent of hot sand and salt, and the sound of the lapping ocean.

Then, with a lingering look around, Daniel Holmes stepped into his own world.

As his feet sank into the sand, he closed his eyes and felt the warmth of the sun on his face.

He was truly happy.

Turning back, he looked to Susan standing on the other side of the door.

"See you around, Susie Feather."

Susan and Mirren kept their eyes on his contented face until the door clicked shut and the doorway disappeared, leaving an inky impression in the air for a moment. Soon that too had vanished, leaving no trace in the world of Daniel Holmes, the second proprietor of the Nowhere Emporium.

Mirren took her mum's hand, and they watched in wonder as the golden letters on the black leather cover of the *Book of Wonders* warped and stretched and separated, forming new shapes, new letters, until they read:

The Wonders of
Susan Feather

"No going back now, Mum," said Mirren.

Susan laughed. "No, I don't suppose there is." She squeezed Mirren's hand. "Come on. Let's get started."

And off they went, hand in hand, to find new adventures.

The Nowhere Emporium will go on forever, I think, as long as it stays in the right hands.

Those were the words of Daniel Holmes. And he was correct. The Emporium's magic will live forever, passed from person to person, as long as imagination exists.

Susan and Mirren Feather are out there now, travelling the world, inviting customers into the shop from nowhere, encouraging them to discover fresh Wonders, fresh imagination. Fresh magic.

One day, Susan too will turn her eye to the future, begin the search to find the right hands into which the Emporium will inevitably pass.

"Oh, it won't be *me*," you might say. "There's nothing special about *me*."

But it has to be *someone*, doesn't it?

It pays to remember, in this world, that magic is imagination. Imagination is magic. And, as Mr Lucien Silver once told Daniel, for those who keep an open mind, those who truly believe, there is treasure everywhere.

So, if one day you happen to come across an old shop made of sparkling black bricks, come on in. Have a look around. Keep an open mind. And above all else...

Bring your imagination.

ACKNOWLEDGEMENTS

Huge thanks to Inclusive Minds for connecting us with their Inclusion Ambassador network, in particular Hannah Hoskins, whose advice was invaluable. I'd also like to thank Debs Bond at the charity Reach for connecting us with members Cathryn and Grace Baker, Anna Hanger and Maria Hutson, whose detailed insights into living with an arm difference helped me to write about Mirren and her experiences.

Thanks as always to my amazing wife Aileen, and my daughters Selina and Mollie. I know it's not always easy putting up with my writing moods and sharing me with the characters in my head. I love you. And to Mum and Dad, as always, for everything.

Five years ago, when *The Nowhere Emporium* made its way tentatively into the world, I could not have imagined the journey that was to follow.

Amazing and unexpected things have happened since then: awards and festivals and school visits, road trips and TV appearances and Blue Peter badges. I am so grateful that I've been able to share these experiences with the fantastic team at Kelpies, particularly my wonderful editor Sally Polson, who makes me look much better than I am, and the brilliant Suzanne Kennedy, who, among an infinite number of other things, has helped me travel the country to meet thousands of eager readers. I've loved every moment.

A million thanks to Steph and Izzy for all you've done every step of the way. The journey continues...

And finally, to those of you who have read and loved the *Emporium* books, who have recommended them and voted for them and made your own Wonders in school and at home, I will never be able to find words big enough to show my gratitude. Thank you all.

Are you brave?

Read on for an exciting extract from
Ross MacKenzie's mysterious and
magical novel *Shadowsmith*...

From the Blue Peter Book Award Winner

SHADOWSMITH

Ross MacKenzie

FROM THE AUTHOR OF
THE NOWHERE EMPORIUM
Ross MacKenzie

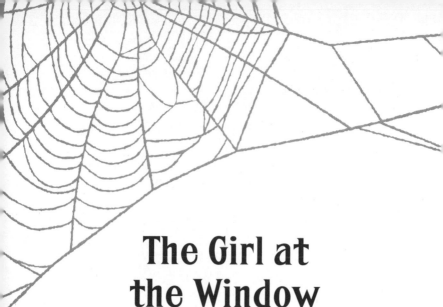

The Girl at the Window

Kirby lay on his bed and stared at the spider on the ceiling.

It's watching me, he thought as the spider twitched its legs. *It's actually watching me.*

The spider was about the size of a fifty pence piece. It was blacker than black, the colour of a nightmare.

And it had been following him.

He knew it sounded mad. But for the last week it seemed like the spider was everywhere he went. Even when he couldn't see it, he could sense it. And when he thought about the spider, inside his head felt like the air just before a rainstorm, heavy and dull and full.

He was beginning to wonder if it was really there

at all. Maybe it was a trick of the mind, his brain's way of distracting him from real life, from the awful thing that was happening to his family.

Two weeks had passed since the storm.

When you lived by the sea you got used to storms. They were a part of life, as normal as shopping or homework or the threat of gull droppings on your ice cream. But this one had been different. Nobody had predicted that such a violent storm would strike at the start of summer. Kirby could still hear the roar of the wind through the winding streets of Craghaven, still see the rain smashing against his classroom window. He could hear his footsteps echo in the empty school corridors and see the frightened look in his dad's eyes as he waited for Kirby in the office.

Two weeks.

The summer holidays had begun since then. His classmates were out playing in the streets or heading off on holiday with their families, full of nervous excitement at the thought of starting high school at the end of the summer. Repair work had begun on the storm-damaged buildings. The world was still turning. Life was going on.

But not for Kirby or his dad.

For them, the world would not turn again until the moment Mum woke up.

The dread of never seeing her smile again, never hearing her voice or feeling one of her hugs had consumed Kirby, filled him up until there was room for nothing else.

Until the spider had arrived.

Clack!

Kirby's gaze left the spider, flicked to the window.

Clack!

He sat up just as another stone – *clack!* – bounced off the window pane.

There was a girl in a yellow plastic raincoat down on the pavement. When she spotted him peering out at her, she smiled and waved, and motioned for him to open the window.

Kirby slid the rickety bottom half of the window upward, letting the fresh sea air into his room. The summer nights were stretching, but it was late enough that the vast sky was turning a dark, rich blue, and the reflection of the moon was molten silver on the waves.

Kirby poked his head out into the night. "Who're you?" he said. Then, trying to sound stern like his dad, he added, "What you playing at?"

"I'm Amelia," said the girl in the raincoat. "Amelia Pigeon. And I'm not playing. I'm not playing at all." Amelia Pigeon half closed her eyes. "Are you brave?"

Kirby frowned. *Am I brave?* What a weird question.

Funny though – he'd been asking himself the same thing a lot lately.

"Dunno," he said. "Hope so."

Amelia Pigeon smiled up at him, all front teeth

and freckles. She looked about twelve, the same age as Kirby. "That's a good answer. Usually I find it's the ones who strut around with their chests puffed out that aren't brave at all. Not when it matters." She tilted her head to one side. "You've seen the spiders, haven't you?"

Kirby's breath caught in his throat. "There's more than one?"

"Course there's more," said Amelia. "When did you see one last?"

"A minute ago. It's gone."

Amelia shook her head. "Not gone. Never gone. Just watching."

"Watching what?"

Amelia scratched her nose. "You. They want *you* gone."

"You do know that's crazy?" said Kirby.

"Think that if you want," said Amelia with a shrug. "Won't make the slightest bit of difference. Can anyone else in your house see them?"

"Don't think so. Dad hates spiders. If he'd seen one I'd have heard him swearing at it or trying to kill it with one of his shoes. When you say they want me gone..."

"Dead," said Amelia matter-of-factly. "They want you dead. I said gone because it sounds less scary."

Kirby was not usually the type of boy to be left stuck for words. But now he thought for a moment and opened his mouth, and all he could say was, "*What*?"

Amelia Pigeon reached into her yellow raincoat, and when she pulled out her hand she was holding a rough, barky twig about the length of a ruler. "Take this," she said, and she tossed it up to the window. Kirby missed it. Amelia Pigeon gave him a sharp look and tossed it again. This time he caught it.

"What is it?"

"Hazel. Picked at midnight. Simple, but it works."

Kirby examined the stick. It looked like every other stick he'd ever seen.

"They'll come soon," said Amelia. "Don't know exactly when. But they'll come. And there'll be lots of 'em."

"Lots of spiders?"

"When they come, use the hazel," Amelia went on. "Like this…" She pulled another twig from the depths of her raincoat, touched the tip to the ground, and drew an imaginary circle around herself. "They won't come inside the circle. Whatever you do, don't step outside it. And don't panic."

"But—"

"I have to go. Things I need to do. I'll be back."

"If you say so," said Kirby. He glanced at the hazel twig in his hand, and when he looked back the girl was gone.

THE STORY CONTINUES IN

SHADOWSMITH

PRAISE FOR THE
NOWHERE EMPORIUM SERIES

'The shop is right up there with Ollivanders as a magical place that readers will want to explore again and again.'
– *The Guardian*

'Storytelling genius; a fantastical, fitting finale to a trilogy I want to climb inside the covers of and never leave. Ross MacKenzie's magical touch makes you believe in the impossible where endless imagination and wonder permeate so perfectly through his pages.'
– Scott Evans, *The Reader Teacher*

'Detailed and original, yet never sacrificing the human story for fantasy, this fabulous book will enchant and inspire.'
– *Book Trust*

'Magical, gripping and imaginative... a delight.'
– *Books for Topics*

'An exciting fantasy with a daredevil sense of urgency.'
– *Foreword Reviews*

'MacKenzie creates a dazzling fantasy world, so engaging and vivid it reminds one of Cornelia Funke's books.'
– *LoveReading4Kids*

'A showmanship of storytelling that will delight all readers.'
– *Mr Ripley's Enchanted Books*

'It is a story that stays with you once you put it down, makes you worry about the characters when you are not reading, and makes you imagine how they lived their lives after that last sentence.'
– *Midnight Readers blogspot*